FEATHERS, FROST & FATE

AN OF FATE NOVELLA

C.A. BLOOMING

Book Cover by @kmdavidsonbooks

Character Art by @avoccatt_art

Map by @studioallred

Editing by Wonder and Wander Publishing

Paperback ISBN: 9798344162942
Hardback ISBN: 9781964087092

This novel has been developed for character, pacing, plot, and emotional appeal by Hyrum M. Allred using a process based on Katherine Farmer's STORY CODE.

Author's Note

Feathers, Frost & Fate is a novella intended for mature readers only (18+). There are topics discussed within this novella that may be upsetting for some readers. Please be sure to take your mental health into consideration prior to reading.

Readers should be aware of the below content:
Childhood trauma and abuse (physical and mental)
References to sexual and physical assault (not on page)
Full sexual scenes

For those who find the courage to be who they are.
Loudly and proudly.

COMAS

Chapter I

One Week After Challenge - Year 4,850 of the Second Age

Jesiel Keita stood at attention beside his Governing God, ready to protect his future King. While observing the room, he watched the celebrations rage on around them.

Roan groaned, "I hate thrones."

Jesiel's gaze glanced to where Roan fidgeted on the obsidian throne kept in the Palace of Nyte. "Then get rid of it," he replied bluntly.

Jesiel bit back his amusement from the glare Roan threw his way. Roan shifted on the throne once more. "I'll get rid of it after this celebration is over."

"If you could call it a celebration," Jesiel muttered.

"Jes, not right now," Roan ordered.

"Why? Don't want your new citizens to know you threw the competition?" Jes challenged.

Roan stood abruptly, and the music around them stopped. He leaned closer, lowering his voice. "You are allowed your opinions and your feelings, but you will keep them to yourself until I'm ready to have a conversation."

Jes met Roan's eyes with squared shoulders. "Is that a command or a request?"

Roan's shoulders slumped forward. "Please, Jes."

Jes nodded his head before turning on his heel. He wasn't going to get into a public argument with Roan. Not when the majority of the Region was in attendance, and not when this was supposed to be a celebration for the new God of Nyte.

But that was just the thing: Roan was never supposed to be the God of Nyte, at least Jesiel didn't believe so. Roan had more power in one thumb than any other Governing God Jes had encountered. He was certainly more powerful than his sniveling, older brother.

Jesiel stepped off the dais, not bothering to glance back at his Governing God.

As he crossed the expansive ballroom, he rolled his eyes at the nonchalant celebrations occurring around him.

Fates, he hated parties.

Slipping through the balcony doors, he made his way out into the fresh air of Iluna. His wings relaxed behind him while he rolled his shoulders, forcing himself to calm his emotions.

"Not enjoying yourself?" a sneering voice came from the shadows.

Jesiel turned on his heel, arms already crossing over his chest when he made eye contact with the God of Wintur—Moros.

"What do you want?" Jesiel snapped.

"Why, *Jesiel—Jes*. Have I done something to bother you?" Moros replied with an irritating grin.

Jesiel stared at the Governing God, fighting his Beskermer nature to lower his head in respect. Because this God didn't deserve an ounce of his respect. Not when he'd obviously chosen the *wrong* side. Not when everything appeared to be a joke to the man.

"I don't have time for your antics tonight, Moros," Jesiel replied, turning back to the balcony. His eyes went up to the brilliant night sky of Nacht.

He couldn't ignore, however, the chilling cold approaching him.

"Those wings are awfully *large*," Moros said with a mischievous tone.

"Well, *Moros*, most Beskermer wings are large," Jes replied, refusing to glance at the God.

Moros laughed and Jesiel focused his eyes on the stars shooting overhead. The sound had sent a shiver down his spine, in a way he'd never experienced before.

Moros's cold shoulder brushed against Jesiel's right wing. His hand gripped the balcony rail in response, fighting back a shocked groan from slipping through his lips.

"Roany is the God of Nyte," Moros sang mockingly.

Jesiel shrugged. "You and I were both at the challenge. I'm not sure why you're stating the obvious."

"Oh, that challenge *was* interesting," Moros replied. Jesiel glanced at him briefly, watching the starlight catch the glistening dark locks of Moros's long hair. "Who knew someone as powerful as Roan could hold himself back so easily?"

FEATHERS, FROST & FATE   9

Jesiel had pounced on the God before he'd realized what he was doing. Every natural instinct in him screamed to protect his bonded from whatever slander threatened to leave Moros's lips.

Moros let out a surprised gasp as they flew across the balcony, slamming into the obsidian walls behind them.

"You watch your tongue, God," Jesiel warned, his face now inches from Moros's.

Brilliant, blue eyes stared back into his own and a gleam lit in the God's gaze. "If you wanted to pin yourself against me, you could have just asked."

Jesiel stepped backward, wiping the dirt from his trousers before straightening his wings out behind him. He watched while Moros shoved away from the wall, unable to take his eyes of the God. A piece of him wanted to believe he watched out of duty—to ensure the nuisance wouldn't pull any more stunts.

But the part of him he kept hidden knew the truth; he watched because he wanted to. Because, despite his attempts to ignore the God's features, he had always noticed them.

The long hair.

The dark skin, only a few shades lighter than his own.

Those blue eyes.

That smile.

Moros cleared his throat. "Something on your mind, Jes?"

Jesiel shook his head, clearing his thoughts. "Only my friends can call me Jes."

"Are we not friends, *Jes?* You are my cousin's bonded Beskermer. Which practically makes you family."

Jes stared while the God inspected his nails nonchalantly, as though he had no idea of the wounds he'd inflicted upon Roan. Which was nearly impossible given the rage Roan went into whenever Moros was mentioned.

"Your loyalties are questionable," Jes replied.

Moros's brows crumpled before he smiled once more. "I do what is best for myself. Is that so wrong?"

Jes studied the God for a moment, ignoring the desire to admire his features longer. "It's wrong when you're hurting people who cared for you. Who would have stood by your side through anything."

Moros rolled his shoulders while his lips pursed into a tight line. Jes watched him, waiting for the inevitable quip he was known to give back.

But he said nothing. The God only stared back with little to no emotions breaking through his expression.

Jes rolled his eyes, turning on his heel. "You can't even explain why you do what you do."

The warm spring air chilled and frost layered over the balcony, creating a slick pathway. Jes turned back to Moros, finding a grin splayed across his face.

Moros flipped back his hair then shrugged. "I don't need to explain myself to a lowly Beskermer. I'm the Governing God of Wintur. I can do whatever I wish."

Rage boiled beneath Jes's skin. His hands balled into fists while he took in deep, grounding breaths. "You and Marek were made to be friends. You're both despicable."

Moros slid across the icy balcony with ease, appearing inches from Jes's face. The God leveled his gaze, squaring his shoulders slightly.

"Isn't it so much more *delicious* to hate someone? To be disgusted by their actions? But..." Moros's hand caressed Jes's bicep, "to also be intrigued by that hate? Why wouldn't you want to see what it could *do?*"

Jes stepped back in shock, slipping on the ice beneath him. The cold of Moros's touch left an irritating trail down his arm, that ignited a burn throughout his body and travelled far lower than Jes was comfortable with.

When he snapped himself out of his daze, his hand gripped Moros's wrist, stopping the God from his teasing touches.

"You keep your hands off me," Jes warned.

Moros's grin lit the blue in his eyes. "Why do you deny yourself pleasures, Jesiel? Does your God prevent you from enjoying yourself?"

Jes glanced back at the party raging behind the balcony doors, finding Roan sitting on the throne again.

With a scowl on his face.

Jes rolled his eyes. They were only here because Roan refused to accept his birthright. Because Roan was so scared to become King, that he threw his shot at actually changing something in their world. At being the good they all needed.

But Jes also knew Roan was terrified and he couldn't fault his closest friend for avoiding his greatest fear. For fearing who he was inside of himself.

Because Jes was intimately familiar with that kind of fear.

Jes turned his gaze back to Moros, finding the God with the same grin on his face.

"Well?" Moros sneered.

Jes threw the God back, watching him slip on his own ice. "I don't deny myself anything, Moros. I know how to enjoy myself whenever I'd like to."

The spring air grew colder. Jes glanced up, finding an approaching cloud, followed by a light sprinkling of snow. Despite his annoyance with Moros for causing a scene, the snow was captivating.

The frigid flakes gently fell on his cheeks, enamoring him with their beauty.

He still wasn't used to it, even though it snowed every Wintur in Nacht. Having grown up in the cool breeze between Spreng and Haust, Jes was always lost in the snow. Unexpectedly finding peace in the silence while it fell. In the chill—burning into his bones. But while his body always begged him to return to the warmth, his soul...

His soul found home in the cold.

Jes turned his eyes from the snow, finding Moros in the middle of the storm, seemingly lost in his own thoughts.

The ice crawled up his dark grey trousers, stopping at his waist. His long hair lifted by some invisible force, flowing like soft dark waves between the stark white flakes falling around him. Moros's hands moved through the snow, and while his wrists flicked around, more fell from him. As though he were made from it.

Jes's warm breath came out in hot puffs before him. He shivered, throwing his arms around his body to bring relief from the freeze. Because he couldn't go back inside now. Not with the beauty occurring before him.

Not with how mystical and otherworldly the God of Wintur appeared before him.

A low laugh warmed his body and Jes blinked, watching the snow die down around Moros. He realized the laugh was coming from the God. The sound had pulled at him, like some kind of string inside of him being tugged on for the first time.

"Did you like my show?" Moros asked.

Jes's hands shook at his sides. "Tonight is Roan's night, Moros. Did you have to make it about yourself?"

Moros's smile dropped. The remaining snow stopped instantly, and the warm breeze returned. "You know I actually came here to warn Roan about something, but I think I'll just excuse myself."

Jes stepped forward. "Warn him about what?"

"Why does it matter now, *Jesiel*? You believe I'm here to harm your Governing God."

"That's my duty, *Moros*," Jes replied.

Moros grinned. "I'm well aware of the Beskermer bond, Jes. Riki makes sure I do not forget. Say, have you spoken to your lovely, little cousin lately? She's rather amazing."

Jes's body locked up at the mention of a family member. It had been a decade since he'd seen any of them. Since he'd allowed himself to speak to anyone with ties to his parents—to his mother.

"Riki did tell me to send her greetings. Don't worry, she doesn't hold your inability to man up to your mother personally." Moros laughed.

Jes snapped, his wings flew out from behind him, and while his Beskermer nature protested, he attacked—again.

He barreled toward Moros, throwing the God across the balcony. His forearm went to Moros's throat, pressing firmly, but not enough to actually take the God's life.

"You know nothing, Moros," Jes said, lowering his voice.

Moros stared up at him, amusement burning in his eyes. But it wasn't just amusement. There was so much more in the stare, enough to send a jolt of need to Jes's cock.

Jes released the God, stepping back abruptly. Running his hand over his jaw, he cleared his throat. "You need to leave, Moros."

"But I was enjoying you holding me down," Moros laughed. "It was more fun than I've had all day."

"What, was whatever debauchery and sick entertainment you partook in with Marek not enough?"

Moros's mood shifted and his shoulders straightened. The God's amused expression hardened. "What I do with Marek is none of your business. If Roan would like to know what his brother is up to, he can ask me personally. We all know the man doesn't deserve the celebrations he's holding."

Jes watched in shock while Moros stormed away, throwing his hair back over his shoulders.

He hated how interested he was in the God. How much of a battle he had to fight inside of himself to not run after him. To console whatever emotions he was feeling. To find out what Marek had done.

Jes sank to the balcony floor, placing his palms over his face. After a moment, he leaned his head back against the obsidian walls of the palace, watching the night sky once more.

They weren't supposed to be there. They weren't supposed to be waiting for the second challenge as though it were this doom of fate lingering over them.

Jes glanced back at the party, finding Roan with a woman on his lap.

Relief rushed through him. At least Roan would find some physical solace to end the night. When they woke, when they had a chance to speak not as Governing God and bonded Beskermer, but as brother to brother...

Jes was going to beat his ass.

Jes turned his head back to the direction Moros had stalked off. His body warming at the thought of Moros's touch against his skin. He cursed himself for not allowing himself to follow the intrigue inside of him. To allow himself his own solace in the hands of the mischievous God. To not follow the desire his body had to do the exact opposite of what he'd been told his entire life.

He closed his eyes while his fingers traced where Moros ran his finger down his bicep. His thoughts took off while the sounds of the party boomed out behind the balcony doors, drowning out any other noise. Allowing him to imagine a night lost in the snow with the God of Wintur.

CHAPTER 2

Moros stalked through the crowded streets of Iluna, his heart racing with both rage and need. His hair that brushed against his back while he walked brought more irritation.

How dare that *Beskermer* talk to him like that? How dare that giant beast believe he could be so callus with a Governing God? He had only come to this dark little Region to inform Roan of his brother's depraved celebrations.

To beg that idiotic coward to actually fight next time.

Moros huffed, brushing through the crowds of celebrating citizens, heading for the Perambulate. He had to get out of this Region. He had to get back home to realign himself.

Nothing he did was ever enough. Or ever seen as serious.

Could he be sterner? Of course. But he'd lived a life under a stern, uncaring hand. He'd seen what allowing status to drive your actions does.

He would never do that. He would never allow himself to believe he was better than another. Or that his status was more than anyone else's.

Well... unless that involved an infuriating Beskermer who refused to accept his place in society.

Moros glanced back at the ominous palace at the outskirts of the city, looming over him like some menacing warning.

He'd always found Jes attractive. When he'd attended Roan's bonding ceremony one-hundred-and-fifty years prior, he'd instantly noticed the towering beast that was Jesiel Keita.

With his monstrous height, broad shoulders, and those captivating golden eyes that illuminated against his dark skin he was impossible to miss. There was also his short-cropped hair and that cut jaw. Jesiel was truly a work of art likely hand-carved by the Fates themselves.

Moros remembered the bonding ceremony fondly. Standing in the blaring heat of Guerra's sun with his own Beskermer, Riki, at his side. Watching in the stands while Eon, the Fate, proclaimed Roan's chosen Beskermer.

Shocking everyone in attendance.

Because while Jesiel was large and terrifying, the expectation had been that Roan would have chosen anyone else. All due to the fact it wasn't common for a child of a Governing God to choose a *friend* as their Beskermer. And that it was even more uncommon for the child of the *King* to do so.

Moros's uncle had screamed out in rage when Roan had declared his bonded. Throwing his head back, slamming his hands on his throne, demanding the Fates to deny the bond.

But Eon did as they wished, and the bond was granted.

Moros had studied the King that day, watched his rage as he glared at his son—at the child he appeared to loath. Only, Moros could see it in his uncle's eyes—the fear. Of what? He wasn't sure exactly.

That was until five days prior when he'd watched his cousin clearly throw the challenge.

Moros walked closer to the Perambulate of Iluna while he pondered the challenge. The little event he thought was silly and unneeded, but the Fates declared it.

So it was. So it has been. So it would always be.

A challenge between the King's two sons. Pitting them against one another to discover whose power was strong enough for one to be declared as King of Gods and one as God of Death. The latter being the "loser" to the majority of the world.

His uncle had always touted Roan's older brother, Marek, as the one to take his throne. As the one to rule the world of Comas. Fates, even Moros himself had believed it. But watching Roan that day at the arena—watching him carefully consider his next move—watching his body physically restrain from showing *too much* power, that had been the most thrilling event Moros had attended in decades.

Enough so, that, after stopping Marek from completing his most depraved desires, Moros had thought coming to Nacht to speak to Roan was the best decision. Because what their world didn't need was another mad man on the throne. They needed someone level-headed. Someone kind.

Moros may have chosen to be Marek's keeper years before, essentially severing any trust Roan had in him, but he now understood Roan was the better choice.

Moros waved his hand, covering the Perambulate building with a thick layer of frost, alerting the citizens of Iluna that he had arrived. Panicked whispers filled the room as he stepped past the queue waiting for the portal. Even if he didn't believe he was better than any person here, he did relish in the status he had with his title.

The respect.

Moros approached the portal, allowing its warmth to overpower his chilling cold. He squared his shoulders with a deep breath, and thought of his Governing God portal, of his beautiful palace of Ice back in Veturs.

Of home.

Moros stepped through the portal at the Palace of Wintur, taking a deep breath of the frigid air. His shoulders finally relaxed once the chill layered over him once more.

His bare arms prickled slightly at the freeze before readjusting to the temperature his body preferred. His hand ran across the ice walls of his palace, while his eyes admired the beauty of his home.

It was magnificent. A towering fortress of ice at the top of the mountain that Kall was built around. The sharp edges of the ice palace acted as a metaphor to leave the God of Wintur alone, but the hearths in his home, and every home in his Region were warm. They were welcoming to any lost travelers or souls searching for a place to rest their heads.

The sound of scuffling pulled his attention from the beauty of his home, and he turned his head, finding his Beskermer standing at attention near his study door.

Moros grinned, throwing his hair back over his shoulder. "I saw your cousin," he laughed.

Riki stiffened slightly before nodding her head. "Not my brother?"

Moros threw her a glance, then shrugged his shoulders. "Arno was busy with some mundane task Marek had forced him to complete."

"How did it go in Iluna?" Riki questioned, her brow raising slightly.

Moros stared at his Beskermer. She was small compared to every other Beskermer he knew. Her tiny frame was almost a mockery of the strength of her kind, but the fire in her golden eyes, those could burn their entire world to ashes.

Riki shook her head, her tight braided locks swaying against each other at the nape of her neck. "Moros?" she asked, crossing her arms over her chest.

Moros laughed, throwing his hand up in indifference while he stepped past his Beskermer. "As expected."

"Were you able to speak to Roan?"

"Roan is Roan. I didn't have a chance to."

Riki scoffed. "So, it was useless then?" Her eyes narrowed. "Why did you speak to Jesiel?"

Jesiel's name came from Riki's lips with a quiet squeak—the only subtle indication of how she felt about her estranged family member.

"Well, Jesiel was brooding on the balcony and for some reason I was intrigued," Moros replied.

"Did you bother him?" Riki demanded, stepping in front of Moros.

"For someone who hasn't done a thing to reach out to the man in over a decade, you sure are touchy that I've had a conversation with him," Moros bit back.

Riki's shoulders sagged with defeat, and with a sigh, she nodded her head. "My aunt... She asks how he is when I visit home."

"She should ask him herself instead of trying to make you her messenger."

Riki's golden glare speared into Moros, but he bit back his laugh. They stood in the hallway for a moment, him towering over her petite frame and her staring him down. When her annoyance had finally cooled, she tilted her head down.

"Sorry," she whispered.

"Stop apologizing, Riki. You can't run this Region as my Beskermer if you're always apologizing for speaking your mind."

Her head snapped upward again before she nodded silently. "I'm not used to this arrangement. Even after all these years."

Moros waved his hand, motioning for Riki to follow him down the hall. "Used to what, exactly? Freedom? The ability to be who you want? Not worrying about what your *Governing God* thinks of you?"

Riki was silent behind him, but Moros knew her well enough after all this time to know he'd hit a sensitive spot for her.

Throwing open the towering icy doors to his throne room, he glanced back at his Beskermer. "You're breaking out of the mold your people tried to put you into. That's something to be proud of, Riki. Stop apologizing for being yourself."

"You're lucky to have had support in your life, Moros," Riki replied quietly.

Moros stopped his steps. The words hit into him like one of the freezing walls of his palace had fallen onto his chest. Balling his hands at his side, he tried to breathe, tried to clear the rage in his heart.

His eyes fell to the blue, frigid throne in the middle of the room. He had grown up loathing that seat, specifically the man who had sat atop it. The disapproving sneer his Father had always given him from his raised throne, staring down at his child with disgust.

Moros turned back to Riki, trying to shake off the memory. "You and I both know I had *half* the support any child should have." He paused, his hand moving to rest on her shoulder. "But that was still double the amount of support you ever had."

Riki's golden eyes glistened with tears before she nodded and shook his hand from her shoulder. Puffing out her chest, she offered him a knowing smile.

"So, my cousin?"

Moros laughed, throwing his hair back behind him. He sauntered to the throne he forced himself to sit upon and leaned his chin onto his palm. "He's fun to pester. Fates, he's even more fun to rile up."

"Don't push him too far, Moros," Riki warned.

Moros chuckled. "I think that large man needs to be pushed more often. He's always so pent up. Always so *stern.*"

Riki shook her head. "You can't blame him. The expectations we all had on us are not easy to shake."

"Yes, but I don't believe for one moment that Roan of all people holds his Beskermer to those fucked up standards you were raised with."

Riki's eyes flared for a moment and Moros wondered if he'd pushed her too far. She cleared her throat, shaking her head. "You are lucky we've lived almost a century bonded together, Moros."

Moros offered her a smile. "But haven't we had so much fun? Think on it, Riki. All the things you've been able to do since the Fates accepted our bond, all the *people* you've been able to experience."

Riki's shocked yell echoed in the room and Moros bit his lip. He thrived in pushing her buttons, in making her realize her strength and forgetting the archaic beliefs the Beskermers held. Because she was the most capable person he'd ever met and having her bonded protection was his life's highest honor.

"You speak so openly about private matters," Riki replied briskly.

Moros laughed. "Riki, your partner of the last several years is hardly a private matter at this point. How are they by the way?"

Riki's eyes were cast downward while a proud smile graced her lips. "Wonderful, as always."

"And your family?"

"Accepting it," Riki snapped.

Moros nodded his head. "That's all I need to know. But if they cause trouble—"

"You'll freeze their balls off," Riki laughed.

"Precisely," Moros replied with a wink.

Leaning back against his throne, Moros let out a heavy breath. His reasonings for going to Iluna had utterly failed, but he hadn't given up hope yet. Not after the depravities he'd stopped earlier that evening, not when he knew the fate of their world rested on Roan's shoulders.

His fingers rubbed his eyelids, circling slowly while his mind reeled. He had to focus on the task at hand. He had to get into his cousin's head. But there was that annoying voice in his mind begging him to *pester* that towering Beskermer further.

His eyes sprang open, the idea igniting inside of him. Perhaps Jesiel was the key to solving everything.

Oh and what a wonderful game he could play.

CHAPTER 3

J es eventually returned to the party, after he'd allowed himself to live out a few forbidden fantasies in his head.

Leaning against the back wall of the ballroom, he scanned the guests, searching for any possible distraction from the tightness low in his back. There were people everywhere. Dancing, laughing, grinding against each other.

But no one truly caught his eye. Not one body had ignited the fire inside of him that Moros left after only a few brief moments alone.

Irritated, he watched as an unfamiliar Godling woman ran her hands across Roan's chest, still sitting atop his lap. But Roan looked uninterested, practically disconnected from his body.

Holding back his laugh, Jes called out through the wind. *Is she not enticing enough for the new God of Nyte?*

Roan jumped on his throne. Jes fell back further into the shadows, watching as Roan searched for him. *She's fine,* he finally replied through the wind. *But I'd rather take Nacht back to the manor and crawl into my bed.*

Let her crawl into bed with you, Jes responded.

Roan was silent and Jes watched from the dark corner as he tapped the woman's shoulder before whispering something in her ear. He'd expected her to take Roan's hand, possibly guiding him out of the room. To his surprise though, she gasped as her cheeks turned bright red, before she rushed out of the room alone.

What in the Fates was that? Jes asked through the wind.

I'm in no mood to find someone to warm my bed, Jes, Roan replied solemnly. *I'm heading back to the manor. Are you coming back with me or staying?*

Jes studied Roan from his quiet hiding place, watching Roan slowly lift himself from the throne. He considered going back to the city, to the manor Roan preferred to live in, but he was still too irritated with him to follow.

I'm going to hang back. Maybe find my own partner to warm my bed, Jes replied, not fully believing his own words.

Roan's laugh echoed throughout the room, causing the noise around them to stop. Every head in the room snapped up to gawk at their Governing God but Roan only waved them away.

"It's been quite a taxing several days for me," his voice boomed out. "I'm going to retire to my home, but please, enjoy yourselves. My uncle can handle any destruction of the palace."

The eyes focusing on Roan quickly turned to his silent Uncle at the back of the room—Aeron, the God of Death.

An eerie cold layered over the room when Aeron's voice filtered through the crowd. "As long as my former palace isn't destroyed *fully*, then no one will meet the wrath of the God of Death."

Jes shook his head with amusement. Aeron was as terrifying as a small insect. At least if you really knew the God. Besides himself and Roan, there were only two other people in the large room who knew the God at that level.

Jes's eyes scanned the room, finding Aeron's Beskermer and partner, Nas, behind him. Then after a bit more searching he found her, tucked in the back, with her hands up in the air while she danced. Lahana—Roan's sister.

The four of them could easily break down Aeron's false image, alerting their world of the soft man who ruled the dead. But that was a task for another day.

Jes smiled, watching Aeron grin at Roan, tilting his head down in approval. Roan mimicked the movement before skirting out of the room.

The Beskermer bond to follow Roan pulled at Jes, but he held back. The one difference between their bond and all others was the respect they had for one another. The understanding they were each their own person and while Jesiel would do anything his bonded asked of him, he knew Roan would never force him into anything against his will.

So, after watching his Governing God slip out of the room and toward the nyte sky he now Governed, Jes waited for a moment before turning his attention back to the party reigniting in the room.

His mind lingered back on Moros's cold touch, his tempting soft hair, and the mischievous smile that had graced the God's lips. Tugging at a feral need inside of him to pull those lips against his own. To run his hands against that cold skin, warming it with his own touch.

Shocked by how lost he was in his lust, Jes didn't register the woman standing before him until her hand brushed against his wings, sending a shiver down his back.

"Has anyone told you your wings look like eagle wings?" she whispered.

Jes blinked, trying to realign his thoughts. "Yes, I am well aware of what my wings look like," he finally replied.

The woman grinned, flipping her dark curls over her shoulder. The movement instantly reminded Jes of Moros.

"I've never been with a Beskermer," she said quietly.

Jes took a step back, allowing himself to admire her. Even though his body begged to return to the fantasies of Moros.

His eyes scanned her from head to toe, taking in that long curly hair. The curves of her body, the dark skin practically glowing under the light of the nyte sky. He took all of her in, forcing his mind to focus on the body before him and not the one he could never have.

The woman's hands fidgeted near her thighs. The movement pulled his eyes from her full chest to the slight blush on her cheeks. Until he was finally staring into her brown eyes.

She was honestly beautiful, and someone he would happily have picked for himself. If only she had approached him on any other night.

"Well?" she asked. Her hand softly laid against his chest and his heart raced in response.

"Well?" he repeated.

She stared at him through her thick lashes, her eyes full of need and desire. "Have you been with a lowly Godling?"

Jes grinned at her temptation, at the sultry way her voice emphasized her words. His hand instinctively ran down her arm, in the same way Moros had trailed down his.

"If you need to know, I prefer Godling partners," he dropped his voice to a whisper.

The woman sucked in a breath before clearing her throat. "Would you like to take me home tonight, Jesiel?"

Jes stared into her eyes and the need burning within her gaze. For a moment, he considered what it made him if he took her home. Did it make him an imposter when his body wanted to go wherever the God of Wintur had disappeared to? Did it make him cruel, knowing he would never give her more than an evening of pleasure?

"I would need to know your name to take you home, woman," he responded, dropping his voice lower. Allowing the need to release his building tension to rise to the surface.

She grinned, her eyes gleaming with the dim light of the room. "Doesn't it make it so much more thrilling if you don't know it?"

A night of fun, that's all she wanted.

Relief flooded through Jes, unspoken permission from the Fates for him to lose himself in the distraction he desired. To feel no guilt in allowing this woman into his bed with zero expectations afterward.

Jes gripped her chin, pulling her lips towards him. "We can't go to *my* bed, woman, but this palace has plenty of empty bedrooms waiting to be filled with your sounds."

Her responding gasp went straight to his cock, awakening the need his body had been fighting all night. Her hands gripped his shirt, pulling him closer to her.

"Lead the way, Beskermer," she whispered against his lips.

Jes gripped her backside, colliding his lips into hers, getting lost in the warmth of them while the party rumbled on behind them.

She was eager, welcoming to his rough kisses. To his demand for more. To his hands pulling at her skin, gripping her curves, trying to find something to keep him grounded.

When he was sure their lips were numb, he pulled away, glancing at the open doors.

"Follow me," he said gruffly, pulling her behind him while he stormed past the grinding bodies.

Jes pulled the woman's dress off, letting it fall to the floor in a crumbled mess. Her body shook each time his hands touched her. It brought out a feral pull within him to plunge himself as deep within her as he could. To release the tension aching at his back and traveling down his legs.

"What do you want?" Jes asked against her neck while his hands wrapped around her waist, traveling to the wetness between her thighs.

Her head threw back against him in response. Her breathless reply causing his cock to jolt in response. "Use me, Beskermer. However you'd like."

It was enough for him.

He flipped her around, pulling her lips against his again. She groaned against him, her breasts brushing against his bare toro, barely above his navel.

For a moment he allowed his mind to wander, to contemplate what Moros's body would feel like against his. Hs body's desire for more returned as the thoughts took over while his body moved on instinct, finding all the places this unknown woman likely wanted to be touched.

He imagined Moros's solid chest against his, knowing the God's chest would touch higher up on his own. He wondered what the warmth of his cock against the God's would be like. What fun it would be to wrap his hands around it and play.

His body jolted at the image of what Moros's hand wrapped around him would feel like. His cock pulsed at the thought, as though his hand was actually working him, pulling his release closer to completion.

Jes lost himself in the fantasy, allowing his mind to venture further and further. Allowing his body to pretend Moros was the one touching him, teasing him.

"Oh my god," the woman gasped, snapping Jes back to reality.

He pulled his lips away, realizing his fingers had found her most sensitive spot and he had been rubbing her in rough repetitive circles. And his mind's imagination of Moros's hand pumping his cock had been no imagination when he glanced down, finding her palm tightly wrapped around him.

"No," she moaned, gripping his wrist, "please don't stop that."

Jes held back his laugh, shaking his head while he led her toward the bed, ensuring his fingers returned to their previous playing.

"Who are you thinking about?" she asked through her moans.

Jes's body froze. He snapped his gaze to her brown eyes, finding amusement within them.

"I don't know what you're talking about." he grumbled.

She laughed before pulling his hand from her. Slowly, she climbed onto the bed, her breasts swaying softly with the movement. The next thing he knew, she was kneeling on the bed, closer to his eye level than she'd been before.

"We mean nothing to one another, Jesiel. You can think about whomever you'd like when you fuck me."

Jes knew he couldn't hide the shock on his face by the grin that cracked across hers. All he could reply with was a question he instantly regretted asking. "How do you know my name?"

The woman's brow crumpled before she shrugged. "Everyone in Iluna knows the name of our God's Beskermer."

Jes nodded in agreement, not wanting to dwell on his grievances with Roan when his body was already cursing him for the interruption.

The woman's breath tickled his neck while her hands wrapped around him again. "Fuck me how you'd like to fuck whoever it is you're thinking about. You have my permission."

Jes's head went back without his control when her fingernail lightly scrapped across his tip, causing his cock to pulse. Her other hand curled around the base of him, and he gasped when she suddenly lowered, wrapping her lips around him.

His hips bucked, shoving himself further into her mouth and she laughed around him. Her hand and mouth moved together, turning his thoughts to a jumbled mess.

After a moment, the cold air brought a shocked gasp from his lips while she returned to her kneeling position.

"How would you like to fuck them, Beskermer?" she asked mischievously.

"I don't know who you are," Jes laughed as he gripped her backside, bringing a loud moan from her lips. "But I think you are exactly what I needed tonight."

Her moans filled the room while his other hand played with her breasts and his lips kissed the sensitive crook of her neck. His hand moved lower, brushing past the curves of her stomach, stopping between her thighs.

When he found how slick she was for him, his body pulled tight, needing to bury himself into the warmth waiting for him.

His hands gripped her hips, flipping her to her stomach in an instant. She cried out in shock, but her arousal was evident in the sound.

"Lift your ass," he said gruffly, slapping her sensitive skin.

She obeyed, opening her legs for him. Jes stared at her, appreciating her beauty before slamming himself deep inside of her.

"Yes!" she yelled out, her hands gripping the sheets of the bed.

Jes held onto her hips, pulling in and out with rough movements. Filling the room with her moans and screams. Each thrust his body wanted deeper, more, harder.

Because despite her warmth and pressure fulfilling his body's need for release, his mind could only do as she had instructed. He thrusted imagining the noises were Moros's. He reached around her, running his fingers across her clit, believing he was stroking Moros's hard cock instead.

He allowed his mind to enjoy what he knew he could never allow himself to have. He lost himself in the desire and the fantasy until he reached his own climax, biting back the desire to scream out the God of Wintur's name.

CHAPTER 4

J es allowed the hot water from the shower to cascade down over his body while he recounted how he'd managed to stay secluded and unbothered at the Palace of Nyte with his mischievous companion for three full days. His companion who had eventually told him her name was Isha, a Godling born in Zomner.

They'd spent their days in the quiet room fucking or sleeping, sometimes calling for the remaining employees Roan hadn't let go to bring them food and drink. But even with the number of times they'd each found release, Jes was still as pent up and frustrated as he'd been when Moros had left him alone on the balcony.

He laid his head against the cool shower marble, trying to focus on Isha's mouth moving against him. Her hands crawled up his torso, but nothing appeared to be working.

Finally pulling away, she laughed. "Have we run your body to exhaustion, Jesiel?"

Jes shoved away from the wall, staring down into her brown eyes. "I think my mind is no longer allowing distraction."

He held his hands up, pulling her from the floor of the shower. Brushing her wet hair from her face, he placed a kiss on her forehead.

"This was fun," he whispered against her skin.

She laughed then laid her hand on his chest. "When I found myself in bed with the God of Nyte's Beskermer, I didn't think that would result in three days of him."

"I have to return to my duties."

She nodded, offering him a knowing smile. "Thank you for the fun, Jesiel. I can't wait to tell everyone I know about how good you are in bed."

Jes's eyes widened before he let out a loud laugh. "Was a I just a conquest for you to achieve?"

Isha opened the shower door, offering him a wink before she stepped out.

"Perhaps we were both only distractions our minds desperately needed."

Jes followed close behind her, picking up the room they had been occupying to the best of his abilities. While Aeron had just moved out of the palace a week ago, Jes wasn't sure whether or not the head housekeeper, Etta, had halted her duties.

Once he and Isha were dressed again, they silently walked through the empty palace. Jes didn't know what to say to her. Was he supposed to thank her?

That felt wrong.

Was he supposed to invite her to stay for another evening of fun?

That also didn't feel right.

His mind raced over what to say when they approached the towering main doors. He glanced nervously at her before offering a tight smile.

Isha's bright eyes lit with amusement. Throwing her head back with a laugh, she rested her hand on his chest once more.

"Jesiel, we're both grown. We owe each other nothing."

He let out a sigh of relief. "I did have a great time."

Isha grinned. "Are you going to run off to whomever you were thinking about the whole time now?"

Jes stepped back, eyes widening with shock. He was doing everything he could to push away the thoughts of Moros. He had failed, obviously, but for her to so openly admit he'd thought of Moros throughout their *entire* time... He didn't know how to reckon with that.

"I don't know who you're referring to," he snapped.

"Well, I hope you give yourself the chance to let go with them," Isha replied, brushing her delicate fingers across his cheek. "You deserve happiness, like we all do."

Jes opened his mouth to respond but stopped when the palace doors flung open. Both he and Isha jumped back, and his wings instinctively wrapped around her.

A loud echoing laugh filled the halls of the palace, bouncing off its obsidian walls.

Jes's alarm lessened, the sound of the laugh filling his body with comfort and familiarity. Pulling his wings from around Isha, he glanced up, finding Lahana standing in the doorway of the palace.

Roan's sister offered him one of her bright grins, throwing her long blonde braid over her shoulder. Her hand landed on her waist, her full lips pursing with her mischievous smile.

"Roan sent me," she said with a wink.

"And?" Jes replied, stepping away from Isha.

"If I had known you were holed up here with someone, I would have *never* agreed."

Isha let out a laugh while she walked toward the palace doors. Barely glancing back at Jes, she threw her hand up over her shoulder. "Thanks for the fun, Beskermer. Good luck with your *duties*."

Jes kept his eyes on Lahana while Isha walked away. When they were finally alone, Lahana slowly turned on her heel, her finger pointing in his face.

"Who was that?" she asked slowly.

"A friend," Jes replied.

Lahana narrowed her eyes, but the growing grin on her lips twitched while she tried to hold her stern expression. Jes bit back his own smile, allowing the Goddess to break first.

"Roan is going to lose his mind when he finds out you've been here with someone. You're never going to hear the end of it."

Jes threw up his hand, interrupting Lahana. "Roan could have come and found me himself."

Lahana's voice dropped to a whisper. "He knows you're upset with him."

Jes turned his gaze out the open palace doors, staring at the little city of Iluna off in the distance. Roan hadn't tried to reach out to him through the wind in the days he'd been holed up in the palace. An obvious sign his Governing God knew an argument was on the horizon.

While Jes appreciated their close bond and viewed Roan more like a brother than anything else, that also came with familial-level arguments. Sometimes leading to physical fights before either of them could come to an agreement or compromise.

I'm coming home, Jes threw to the wind.

Lahana jumped beside him, saying nothing despite him knowing her connection to the wind had allowed her to hear his words.

There was silence—enough for Jes to confirm Roan had heard him.

Stepping forward, Jes walked through the open doors, ready to have a war of words with his brother.

Because somebody had to beat the idiot back into sensibility.

Jes slammed the manor doors open, ignoring Lahana's shocked gasp behind him. His eyes turned to Roan's closed study door. In one moment, he puffed his chest out and burst into the room.

Roan startled in his chair before his shocked expression turned to amusement. "Angry, Jesiel?" he asked.

Jes scoffed, irritated Roan was using his emotion sensing so callously. As though he didn't care this magic was only reserved for the one with Kingly powers.

"I would think only a future *King* should be able to sense my emotions," Jes snapped back.

Roan was silent, only his eyes narrowing told Jes he was carefully considering his response.

"Maybe he will," Roan finally replied.

Jes tossed his head back with a laugh, throwing himself in the chair opposite of Roan. "You think your *brother* has that power? Have you started drowning yourself in tonics without telling me? I can't think of anything else that would dampen that usually sharp mind of yours."

Roan's blue eyes narrowed again before he leaned back in his own chair. Jes calmed himself while he considered what to say next. Roan's temper was at times uncontrollable and unleashing it too soon wouldn't be the most logical choice. With relaxed shoulders, Jes turned his gaze to the top of Roan's desk, where a pile of papers sat before him.

"How's running the Region?" Jes pried.

"What—" Roan's question stopped mid-sentence. Slowly, his head snapped up from where he'd been staring at the papers. A grin spread across his face. "Why are you in here, Jes?"

Jes stood. "I can either kick your ass in here—" He paused, pointing out the study doors. "Or the training room. Your choice."

Jes was out the door before Roan could reply, knowing he was baiting his friend. Knowing Roan rarely backed down from a challenge.

Usually.

Slamming open the training room doors, Jes turned to the wardpad. He stared at the small knob before him and twisted it quickly, pulling the pin from its hidden place. He only had seconds before Roan would be in the room. Seconds before this fight he'd taunted would begin and he needed the element of surprise.

Pricking his finger, he breathed through the brief shock, calling his magic to the surface. The room lit with that familiar electric air right before the wards followed their silent command.

Jes wiped the bead of blood from his finger on his pant leg, watching. All around him, the empty room became an indoor replica of the arena Roan had been competing in just days prior.

"What the fuck is this?" Roan yelled out from the doorway.

Jes turned on his heel, throwing the dirt that now covered the ground in Roan's direction.

"We're going to replicate your challenge, Roan. And you're going to tell me why you threw it."

Roan collided with him instantly, sending Jes across the floor into the wall behind him. Jes's head hit the solid surface, sending a shock through him, but not pain. Because he was a Beskermer after all, and it took much more than an angry little God to injure him.

His hand caught Roan's balled fist before it collided with his jaw. "Fight fairly, Roan," he laughed, throwing Roan off.

Roan landed on his feet, his chest heaving. Jes tried not to relish in the brief victory, pushing down the desire to mock Roan for his temper.

"I don't know what you're talking about," Roan muttered.

"You're a bad liar," Jes replied. "You forget I've been your best friend for much longer than I've been your bonded Beskermer."

Roan's hands trembled beside him and Jes held back. There was a fine line between taunting Roan and pushing the God to the point of regret.

The dirt around them lifted the further Roan's body trembled. The air in the room grew electric and Jes held his stance.

Roan was calling forward all the festering power inside of him. Even if it appeared to be outside of his control.

"Why?" Jes asked over the loud hum filling the room. "Why didn't you fight?"

Roan shook his head. "I can't—" He sank to the ground, the dirt encircling him. "I can't become *Him.*"

Understanding settled over Jes while he approached. Standing before his friend, he offered his hand, pulling Roan back to his feet. "You won't, Roan. You can't."

The electric air lessened and the dirt settled beneath their feet as Roan's tear-filled eyes met Jes's gaze.

"It lives inside of me, Jes. This festering poison boiling and burning in my veins. This rage..." he took a breath. "this rage I can't control. This hate gripping my heart."

Roan's hands gestured out to the training room. "This replica of the arena is just a reminder of what I can't do. He's *vile* and demented. So much more than I ever allowed myself to believe. How do you expect me to not fear becoming Him when His blood, this poison, runs through mine?"

Jes held his composure, slipping into his place as Roan's Beskermer. A guiding protective hand to his Governing God.

"You have control of yourself. You can do everything to stop that from happening."

"I don't deserve your friendship," Roan replied, stepping toward the middle of the room. "Your loyalty and support mean the world to me."

Jes stiffened as the words left Roan's lips.

Loyalty.

His curse, bred into him. The one trait he wasn't sure was a strength or weakness.

Roan's hand ran over his hair while he scanned the room. With a snap of his fingers his magic grabbed hold of the wards from the wardpad, tumbling down the magic Jes had set. The training room returned to its previous barren state.

With a grin, Roan turned back to Jes. "You were gone for several days."

"Yes," Jes replied tightly, rolling his shoulders. "What of it?"

"It seems you actually did find someone to *warm* your bed." Roan laughed. "Good for you. You need to let lose more often."

Jes nodded his head. The tugging Beskermer command coiling around him to speak up.

Digging his heels into the ground, he cleared his throat.

"I have to tell you something."

Roan's shoulders slumped. "Way to ruin the brief moment of calm amongst this insane storm." he met Jes's gaze. "What is it?"

Jes's body cooled while his mind went back to the God of Wintur and his surprise visit. Not allowing the conflict of emotions inside of him to slip past his mask, he stared back at Roan blankly.

"Moros was here."

Roan groaned, his irritation obvious across his face. "What in the fucking Fates did he want?"

"He knows you threw the challenge," Jes replied.

Flames erupted from Roan's palms while the room shook around them. "He doesn't know anything!" Roan yelled, throwing fiery balls of rage out into the room.

Jes stepped forward, placing a hand on Roan's shoulder, grounding his Governing God. Bringing him back from the storm inside of him.

"He won't do anything."

Roan whirled around, slapping away Jes's palm. "He's *Marek's* little lacky. Following my brother around like an animal begging for scrapes. Indulging in his depraved parties and celebrations. What makes you think he won't go running to my Father the first chance this knowledge suits him?"

Jes laughed. "Come one, Roan. You and I both know your Father already saw what we all saw in that arena."

Roan scoffed. "He's an issue, Jes. Just him brazenly coming to *my* Region to throw this in my face proves he cannot be trusted."

Jes nodded, his hands balling at his sides.

Roan let out a breath, shaking his head. "He's a traitor, Jes. He always will be."

"Yes, My Lord," Jes replied, not bothering to acknowledge the responding laugh from Roan due to his formality.

Because his heart had twinged at the word *traitor*. A deep part of him fought against the harshness of the term. A part of him that wondered, if perhaps, the God of Wintur wasn't all he made himself out to be.

CHAPTER 5
TWO MONTHS AFTER CHALLENGE

Moros rubbed his fingers over his temple, staring at the papers on his desk with disdain. He let out a groan and leaned into his chair. He hated the mundane tasks that came with Governing Godhood. The approvals requiring his signature. The petty arguments his citizens brought to him.

It was all so irritating.

He crossed his legs, turning his head to gaze to the window in his study. The snow fell softly onto the mountainside, covering Kall with its beauty. Only a sprinkling though, with his season still months from beginning.

He got lost in the beauty of it when his study door creaked open.

"Yes, Riki?" he asked, not turning his gaze to meet his Beskermer's eyes. She cleared her voice. A stern noise that finally pulled his attention.

"Is everything well?"

Riki nodded her head then shuffled her feet.

Moros rolled his eyes. "Riki, either get out with it or get out of this room."

"Marek."

Moros sat straighter, placing his hands on his desk at the mention of his cousin. He let out a breath, trying to appear unphased.

"What about him?"

Riki's hand came from behind her back, and she held up a scroll. Moros's shoulders relaxed, only slightly. His cousin was likely having another one of his rowdy parties.

"Did he summon me personally?" Moros asked.

Riki nodded. "Yes. The parchment just arrived with the messenger. Marek expects your attendance immediately."

Moros stared up at the bright sun in the sky. "It is barely mid-day."

"Marek expects your attendance immediately, your grace," Riki repeated.

Moros shoved away from his desk and let out a heavy sigh. "I suppose I should abide by the prince's request then, shouldn't I?"

Riki's hand went over her mouth and Moros grinned at her struggle to contain her responding laugh.

He turned on his heel, twisting his body to face his barely-visible governing god portal. For a moment he considered ignoring his cousin, but it was brief. Because Moros knew what a mid-day party in Solim likely meant; Marek was bored, and his boredom was usually accompanied by wreckage.

"Don't let things fall to the depths," Moros called over his shoulder while he flipped his hair back.

"That's your job!" Riki yelled back.

Moros shook his head with amusement while he approached the warmth of the portal. He squared his shoulder while his mind went to Solim and the Governing God who ruled the city and Region of Sunne. The portal temperature grew hotter while Moros allowed his thoughts to guide the magic to his destination.

Without looking back at his beloved snow, Moros stepped through the portal when the white palace of Sunne appeared. He fisted his hands at his side, cursing the sweltering heat waiting for him.

"Moros!"

Marek's voice was the first sound Moros heard when his foot touched the other side. He jolted in shock from the quick temperature change and panted from the heat.

"Fates, cousin," Moros groaned, straightening himself. "I do not understand how you enjoy this."

Marek grinned from the large armchair he lounged on. Moros kept his eyes on his cousin, ignoring the quiet woman sitting to the side. Marek was so similar to his younger brother, but also vastly different. Their statures similar, tall but not towering. Both with blue eyes, but while Roan's were a lighter shade, Marek's were a dark blue. Like the deepest depths of the ocean.

Ironically every part of Marek's physical appearance was darker than his brother's. Possibly a symbol of the mark on his soul that Moros had chosen to ignore throughout their lives.

"Isn't she beautiful?" Marek asked with a grin motioning to the woman with his fingers.

Moros held his tongue. He knew exactly who this woman was. This young, foolish, naive Goddess. Aila—the daughter of the current God of War.

Aila sat on the arm of Marek's chair and his hand wrapped her waist in a predatory sign of ownership. Moros bit the inside of his cheek, his mind instantly piecing together how to get the poor woman out of Marek's grasp.

"Riki said you required my immediate audience?" he asked.

Marek's eyes went dark, and he gripped Aila tighter. "We have an issue, Moros."

Moros crossed the room, settling into the chair opposite of his cousin. He crossed his leg and lifted his hand to inspect his nails. Letting Marek know just how *important* he believed this issue to be.

Marek clicked his tongue with annoyance while Moros chose to be silent. Finally, Moros threw his hair over his shoulder and grinned.

"What's the issue?"

"My brother," Marek sneered.

"Roany is a child," Moros replied. "You won, Marek. Why is he still an issue?"

Moros watched while Marek dug his fingers into Aila's side. The Goddess barely flinched, but her eyes could not hide the pain that flashed through her gaze. Marek held onto her while he let out a breath.

"It's an *issue* because I said it is, Moros. What the fuck is your problem?"

Moros grinned. "I have no problem. Just don't understand why you continue to feel threatened by your *baby* brother."

Marek's hand gripping the other arm of his chair grew bright and the room warmed around them. Suffocating Moros with the heat.

"That pathetic coward is worthless," Marek sneered. "He's a terrified child hiding out in Nacht, refusing to accept blame for his *actions*. I want to ensure he is not a threat to me. Is that so wrong?"

Aila whimpered and Marek's gaze pulled from Moros's. Moros sat straighter in the chair, eyeing his cousin while he pulled his nails from Aila's skin.

"My sweet," he whispered. "I apologize."

Aila's back was stiff, her chin high. A woman determined to hold herself confidently, even though Moros could feel her fear from where he sat.

"I must excuse myself, my Lord," she muttered. "My father will wonder where I have been."

Marek grunted, waving his hand in the air with indifference while he leaned back on his chair as Aila stood.

"Tell him the prince thanks him for the company his daughter provided."

Moros's eyes went wide at his open mocking of the woman. Aila's face twisted with shame before she threw Moros a glare then bowed her head.

"Yes, my Lord. Thank you."

Moros was livid, watching while she stepped backward out of the room, leaving the two men alone.

"Do you have to be so fucking disgusting?" Moros snapped.

Marek's smile was predatory, and he leaned his elbows on his knees. "Does it bother you, Moros? Tell me how is *she*? Did you get her home to Veturs in one piece?"

The room layered with Moros's frost while his rage ignited. He stood instantly, pointing his finger in Marek's face.

"I don't give a shit if you're now the Governing God of Sunne, Marek. You will treat me as the elder God who will be respected."

Marek shrugged. "You're tiresome, Moros. Leave me. I thought I was calling my cousin for some entertainment would be worthwhile but you're as melancholy as my brother."

Moros scoffed and threw his hair over his shoulder. He walked back to the portal at the other side of the room then offered Marek an amused smile.

"You know, Marek. That challenge was interesting."

Marek's shoulders went rigid, and he turned slowly to meet Moros's eyes.

"And?" he said slowly.

Moros shrugged.

"I'm curious to see how the next one plays out."

Moros stepped backward, allowing the portal to envelope him before Marek could respond. His mind went to his plans, his cousin, and that frustrating Beskermer he could not rid his mind of.

Despite where his mind had gone, he had expected to go back home. Not to arrive in the Perambulate of Iluna, with Roan's manor off in the distance behind the glass doors.

He wasn't upset though. Roan's Region meant one thing: seeing Jesiel Keita again.

Moros grinned. It would be worth whatever upset he was about to cause.

CHAPTER 6

M oros sauntered through the streets of Iluna. The people of Roan's Region whispered and pointed as he passed their little storefronts. The awe over the Governing God visiting their quaint little Region was enough thrill that he considered staying in the city, avoiding his cousin's Manor on the hill.

His hands moved lazily at his sides while he stopped to admire the tailor's shop before him. Then the sun darkened, and he felt it—the power radiating from the man who shouldn't have even a sliver of that strength.

Moros stared back his reflection.

"Hello, cousin," he said with a sneer.

"What are you doing here?" Roan demanded.

"Interesting that I knew you were approaching before you made yourself known." Moros turned on his heel, offering Roan a knowing grin. "My, whatever would your Father say?"

Roan glared back at him. The freckles lining his face scrunching with his irritated expression.

"What are you doing here?" he repeated.

"Avoiding questions," Moros sighed, flipping his hair over his shoulder. "Always avoiding the difficult things aren't you, *Roany?*"

Roan scoffed. "We both know who avoids things. Please answer my question before I lose my patience."

"Oh, we wouldn't want that to happen, now would we?" Moros replied with a wink.

Roan stiffened, the muscle in his jaw tightening. Moros observed his cousin and the response. Little indications his biting words were true.

"I came to see how the last couple months of being a Governing God has been," Moros said, breaking the silence. Knowing he was lying. That his visit with Marek had unintentionally sent him to Roan's Region.

Ignoring Roan's rolling eyes, Moros continued up the street, toward where Roan's home sat on the other side of the city. The people of Iluna kept their eyes on him, while darting back to the Governing God Moros knew angrily stalked behind him.

Moros grinned. He loved the customs they were all held to. The fact he'd been a Governing God for much longer than his little cousin meant that his cousin had to show respect. Not questioning Moros in public. Giving the elder Governing God the chance to walk ahead—even in his own Region.

Moros pranced through the street, smiling at the shocked faces he passed. These quiet little citizens had no idea how the world worked after having lived under Aeron's thumb for Millenia.

Sad, really, when so much change had occurred during the Reign of their King. But Aeron had led them all in fear, their God of Death acting as the God of Nyte.

Until two months ago.

Moros reached the lawn of Roan's beloved manor, and he glanced backward. Roan hadn't noticed and Moros choked back his laugh at the quiet curses coming from his cousin.

"Upset about something?" he asked.

Roan's head snapped up, his hands balled together at his side. "We're out of the public eye. Tell me why you're here."

"Moros!" a shriek came from the front doors and they both turned to the watch a flash of bright blue rush toward them.

Lahana.

Moros smiled at Roan's younger sister, his heart tightening. She ran down the lawn, her long golden hair flying freely behind her back while her flowing blue gown whipped around her.

He adored his youngest cousin. Honestly, he was sure there wasn't a person in their world who didn't love the bright light that was the Princess. She was the calm amongst the storm of their constantly conflicted world.

Lahana collided into his open arms, and he swung her around, their long hair whipping in the wind Lahana sent around them.

"He's going to beat the shit out of you," Lahana whispered, blocking her words from Roan.

"Let him at me," Moros winked.

He set her down while her wind died down. Both turned to find Roan standing with his arms crossed and surprisingly, a bright crown of stars hovering above his head.

"That's new," Moros pointed.

Roan shrugged. "Still not used to it. Moros, what in the Fates do you want?"

Moros glanced at Lahana, his minding quickly trying to piece together his excuse. Because in reality, he'd found himself wandering to Nacht without his control. His mind focused only on one being.

His eyes lifted to the sky, and he wondered if Jesiel Keita was up there—observing.

"Well?" Roan asked impatiently.

"I want to take my cousin out," he replied, grasping Lahana's hand.

Lahana gasped beside him while Roan eyed them suspiciously.

"I'm not her keeper," he finally said, stepping aside.

Lahana grinned at Moros, the glee in her eyes almost broke him knowing the years she'd been kept in solitude. Grabbing her hand, he pulled her forward when Roan blocked their path.

"But..."

Moros knew he was approaching before Roan could finish his sentence. That tug inside of him, the cold tether that had been called him to Jesiel that evening on the roof yanked inside of him. Slowly, he turned, meeting those intoxicating golden eyes.

Jesiel stood on the front porch with an emotionless expression on his face. But Moros scanned his eyes over him, noting the fists shaking at the Beskermer's side.

The man—the beast—the predator that was Jesiel was just as breathtaking as Moros had remembered.

His towering frame barely made it through the doorway of Roan's manor doors. His multi-colored wings always at attention behind him. His dark skin—Moros was absolutely enamored by that dark skin.

And then there were those golden eyes. The eyes that hid so much. The eyes that stared right back into Moros's soul and he wondered what secrets he could pry from those full lips.

Moros was lost in his admiration when he realized Jes was approaching or stalking toward him and his cousins.

"Jes is going to join you," Roan said behind them.

"Roany!" Lahana protested. "Come on, I'm a grown woman."

Moros grinned at Jes, offering a wink before he turned his gaze to his cousins.

"Do you think I'd harm our precious Na-Na, Roan?" he asked.

"I think I'm the one she followed from Erde and I'm now responsible for her safety. We both know you have shown little regard to a woman's safety before."

Frost licked at Moros's fingers from the challenge lingering on his cousin's tongue. His eyes went back to Lahana's green gaze, finding her staring with concern.

"What is he talking about?" she questioned.

"Nothing," Moros replied, flipping his hair over his shoulder. "Roan knows nothing, which isn't new. What do you say, Lahana? A night out?"

Lahana glanced nervously at her brother. Her fingers tapped at her side and Moros rolled his eyes. She'd been taught, like every other woman in their world to wait for a man's approval.

Thank the Fates, however, Moros knew enough about Roan to know he would never seek to control her wild heart.

"Lahana," Roan's tone turned soft. "You don't require my approval. Go have fun. I have to meet with Aeron anyway."

"Oh, how is uncle?" Moros grinned, cutting Roan off. "I didn't get to say my hellos at your party."

Roan opened his mouth, when surprisingly Jes interrupted. "My Lord, I'll happily accompany these two wherever they're determined to wreak havoc."

Roan shook his head while his hand ran through his hair. "Alright, then."

Without saying another word, Roan passed by, and Moros watched as the new God of Nyte's shoulders sank. For a moment, Moros wondered if he should follow. If his plan to get close to the Beskermer was foolish and perhaps he should have tried the old way: apologizing.

Only...

Moros turned back to where Jesiel stared at him intently, those fists still balled at his side.

Pestering the Beskermer was so much more fun.

"She's enjoying herself," Moros said quietly, watching Lahana dance to the music in the small bar they'd wandered into.

Jesiel grunted beside him. Moros turned his head watching the Besker-mer throw back the dark liquor in his glass.

"Trying to drown out your sorrows?" Moros asked with a laugh.

Jes's glass landed on the table, rocking the surface with the force.

"Why are you here, Moros?" he asked.

Moros stared into his eyes, the golden captivating him. The music drowned out around them while he considered his words. How carefully he had to tread.

"I have my reasons," he finally replied.

Jesiel's head threw back with a loud laugh that echoed throughout the close space. Bodies stopped dancing and heads turned their way, eyes wide.

"You're funny," Jes laughed, slapping Moros's shoulder.

Moros stood, throwing Jes's hand away from him. "Thank you." He tilted into a low bow, his hair falling over his chest.

When he lifted his eyes, he found Jes staring at him. His hands gripped his empty glass but his chest—it was barely moving.

Mission accomplished.

Moros straightened, turning his gaze back to his cousin dancing in the middle of the room. He grinned while he watched a tall blue-skinned Godling woman wrap her arms around Lahana's neck, followed by Lahana's infectious laugh floating through the breeze in the room.

Even if he had come to pester the unmoving brute before him, his quick thinking had been beneficial. He'd gotten that woman out of that manor with the brooding brother she was determined to protect. He'd given her a few hours of freedom. Which was enough of an accomplishment for him to leave right then and there. Leaving her with her companion to dance the night away.

Moros turned back to Jes, and with a wink, stepped backward.

Jesiel stood from his seat and the stool crashed to the sticky ground of the bar.

"Get back here!" he called out.

But Moros had picked up his pace, heading right for the door, toward the quiet streets of the little town they'd ventured into.

"Moros!" Jes bellowed.

Moros reveled in the sound of his name on the giant's lips. It was like a poison, tempting and dangerous all at once.

Moros shoved the door open, sprinting for the cobbled streets, his eyes instantly distracted by the bright nyte sky above. How so much beauty could exist in such a secluded Region was beyond him.

Shaking off his admiration, he ran down the streets, grateful this little town had gone to bed hours before. Unlike the city of Iluna where Roan was probably pouting in his study, overlooking his main city.

Moros's long trousers dragged against the town's roads while he ran down the street, holding in his laughs. He had to get Jesiel away from prying eyes. He had to get him alone.

For what?

He wasn't sure yet.

Moros kept running until he reached the end of the main road, twisting back to glance at the bar at the end of the street. But there was no large body chasing after him. No gruff voice calling out his name in a rage.

His lips turned down with his disappointed frown. Maybe he'd misjudged the Beskermer. Maybe the large man wasn't as intrigued by him as he'd thought.

Moros's turned his attention to the town's little Perambulate when the wind picked up the ends of his hair.

There he is.

His eyes shot upward, finding the dark spot in the sky. The large wings fanned out, creating a majestic silhouette above.

Then Jesiel was before him, the force of his wings beating picked up dirt around them.

Moros couldn't move while the towering body approached. His breath caught in his lungs.

"What is your agenda?" Jesiel demanded. His finger pointed in Moros's face.

"Who says I have one?" Moros countered with a sly grin.

Jesiel stalked closer, his finger dangerously close to Moros's lips.

"Tell me one thing that's true, Moros and I may not believe you to be a constant threat."

Moros stared at him. It was though the air had been knocked out of his lungs. Such a simple request. One that shouldn't have left him so shaken.

"I—" The words stuck in his throat.

"Just what I thought." Jesiel laughed, turning on his heel. "Go home, Moros. Leave us alone and go back to your fucked up friend in Solim."

Moros watched Jes's wings block out the image of the town beyond while he walked away. His head held high as though in triumph. His hands shook at his side as he gathered the strength.

One true thing. He could do that.

All plans, all scheming, melted away while he watched, and he cursed himself before the words left his lips. Because the moment he admitted them. The moment he opened up that part of himself—it was all over.

"I haven't stopped thinking about you since that nyte on the balcony," he yelled out.

Jes's body stopped, and he stilled in that unnatural way only his kin were capable of. Then he launched his body into the sky and Moros was sure he'd lost track of him.

Until his muscled body was slamming into the earth before him, his eyes wide, his chest heaving.

"What did you say?" he whispered.

Moros stared into his golden eyes, fear coursing through his body.

"Follow me. I want to show you something," he replied.

Jesiel blinked, stepping aside as Moros took off toward the Perambulate building.

He couldn't have this conversation is one of Roan's barely populated towns. He couldn't have it out in the open. No, he needed to go to his one place of safety and something, maybe the Fates, was telling him Jesiel was someone he could trust to take there.

His hands threw the Perambulate door open and he ran to the portal. He turned back, watching Jesiel hesitatingly enter the room. His eyes scanning the empty building for any prying eyes.

"Follow me," Moros called out, his hand reaching for the Beskermer while his soul begged the man to follow on this adventure.

To follow him—wherever that would take them.

CHAPTER 7

J es followed Moros through the portal nervously, his hands clasped together to keep them from shaking. With a brief backwards glance, he imaged Roan's disapproving glare holding his gaze. The disappointment his bonded would feel knowing Jes was sneaking out like an adolescent.

And leaving his sister almost completely alone in one of the lesser-known towns in the Region. Jes glanced back through the doors, his eyes finding the little bar they'd spent the evening in, and he realized Lahana was fine.

Even if Roan would rage that Jes was with the only other man he hated besides his own brother.

But the thrill it ignited something inside of Jes—he hadn't felt so alive in his long life.

"Follow me, Jesiel," Moros said tauntingly.

Jes's head snapped back to the God of Wintur, heat rising to his cheeks from the mischievous smile across the God's face.

Moros's long hair swayed while the chill of Veturs filled the air. Jes shivered, wrapping his arms around his body. His head whipped around in confusion when his foot hit the clear ice floors of the Palace of Wintur. He'd expected the Perambulate in Kall, not the Governing God's personal home.

"What magic do you have?" Jes asked quietly.

Moros threw his head back with his laugh. "Glad to hear you believe I'm that *powerful,* Jes."

Jes frowned, annoyance coiling inside at the way he reacted to his name on Moros's lips. "What is this?" he questioned again.

Moros winked. "The Governing God portal, Jesiel. We all have one. Haven't you used Aeron's—or now, Roan's?"

Jes shook his head, lowering his head in shame. Yet another reminder he was going against every instinct he had as a Beskermer. Only, there was another instinct driving his need to follow this God. It wasn't protection for Roan. It was curiosity. It was a need to be near the icy man as often as he could.

Despite the shame that gripped him when he was.

"Interesting," Moros muttered before motioning for Jes to continue following behind him.

Jes picked up his pace, amazed that his feet didn't slip on the ice below him. Allowing his nerves to retreat, he finally observed Moros's beloved home.

His heart tugged at the beauty of it. The ice that made up the palace. The clear ceilings where snow landed softly above. The large windows overlooking the mountain-side town of Kall.

Stopping briefly, Jes gazed out the windows, studying the quiet little city. The snow-capped roofs and the children shrieking in the white powder below.

"There's something serene about it, isn't there?" Moros whispered beside him.

Jes nodded. "There's no snow back home."

Moros chuckled beside him. "I'm very aware of that. If only the Fates would allow you Beskermers to experience it when you're young. I have a theory it would make you all much less melancholy."

Jes turned to face Moros, irritation at the tip of his tongue. But when he met the God's eyes, his body warmed in response. As though the snow outside and the freeze surrounding them didn't exist. Like some unseen heat had infiltrated their space, creating a palpable shift in temperature that only they seemed to be aware of.

Dipping his chin, Jes cleared his throat. "You wanted to show me something?"

Moros's grin spread across his face. "How well do your wings work in the cold? I've heard Beskermers have *performance* issues with temperature shifts."

Jes's eyes widened at the brazen comment. Squaring his shoulders he allowed a sly grin to creep across his lips.

"Would you like to *find out*?" he challenged.

Moros responded with his own mischievous grin, sending a shock of desire down Jes's spine. As he turned on his heal, Moros thew his hand out, gesturing for Jes to follow him. "Outside, Beskermer. Let's go."

Jes's grin grew as he followed the God, ready for whatever unspoken adventure that lay at their fingertips.

They walked through Moros's quiet palace at a brisk pace. Every now and then Moros would throw his hair over his shoulder. Then flip it back to the other shoulder.

Jes watched the movement, curious at how often Moros repeated it. So often, Jes wondered if Moros was aware he was doing it. Jes held back his laugh at how similar it was to Roan's nervous tell of running his hand through his hair.

Lost in his thoughts of admiring the man before him, Jes didn't realize Moros had stopped walking. Until he slammed right into his back.

Moros whipped around, mischief sparkling in his eyes. "Yes, *Jesiel?*"

Jes cleared his throat, fanning his wings out behind him. "I was distracted."

"My ass does do that to others," Moros quipped.

Jes bit his lip, holding in the laugh building in his throat.

Moros winked. "I appear to render you speechless quite often."

"Your jests are not worth responding to," Jes replied coldly, crossing his arms.

Moros's smile faltered for a moment before he offered an unphased shrug. "I'm not the one missing out on the fun, Jesiel."

"Where are you leading me, Moros?"

Moros sighed, flipping his hair once more. "Why did you follow me here?"

Jes opened his mouth before closing it again quickly. Stepping back, he let out a breath. He wasn't sure why he followed Moros. There had been a buzz in the air when he'd followed Moros back to the Perambulate. A beckoning for him to go on an adventure for himself, forgetting any duty he was bound to.

Clearing his throat, Jes shrugged. "I'm not sure."

"You are just as bad as my cousin at answering questions," Moros scoffed.

Jes narrowed his eyes. "Why are you so intent on bothering Roan lately? I thought your relationship was better off at a distance."

"Is that why you followed me? To make sure I don't hurt your precious best friend?" Moros snapped.

"I don't care what you just admitted to me in Nacht," Jes replied, trying to push down his building anger. "But you've done enough to damage what's between you and Roan. There is no friendship in my life that's more important than his and I won't let you get under his skin."

Cold air rushed around them, and Moros was before him in an instant, the tip of his nose brushing against Jes's own. "Would you like me to get under your *skin*, Jesiel?" he whispered.

Jes pushed him back, rage unleashing without his control. "What is wrong with you?" he yelled. "Can you not have a conversation with someone without making it about what your *body* can do for them?"

Moros stared back at him blankly, flipping his hair to the other shoulder quickly.

Jes let out a yell of frustration, his hands landing against his thighs. "Will you stop that? Do you need something to tie your hair back? Cut it for Fates' sake if it's that irritating!"

The echo of his shout rang out down the hall behind them, and they sat there, staring at each other. Jes's hands balled to fists at his side. He hated the emotions Moros brought out in him. Hated how somehow everything this God did rubbed him wrong, while also making him so intriguing Jes couldn't help but think about him.

Moros's chin lifted with indifference before he turned back on his heel. A loud *creak* filled the hall, and frigid air came from the door Jes hadn't realized they'd been standing before.

"Let's go for a flight, shall we, Jesiel?"

Jes rolled his eyes. "Where?" he demanded.

Moros glanced back at him, offering him a wink. "Somewhere special. Will those wings work?"

Jes shoved Moros to the side, stepping out into the freezing air of Veturs. "Get your ass over here and find out."

Jes watched the God approach him, hearting hammering in his chest as Moros grew closer. His hands trembled at his side when Moros stood before him, placing a hand on his chest.

"I have to admit something," Moros whispered, meeting Jes's gaze.

"What?" Jes grunted, jolting at the shock of Moros's touch.

"I don't know how to fly with a Beskermer. Riki is too small."

Jes's breath hitched in his throat while he tried to form his response. Shaking off his irritating reaction, he squared his shoulders. "Put your arms around my neck."

Moros didn't pull his gaze away from Jes's, igniting a rush of need through Jes's body. Slowly, Moros lifted his arms, wrapping them softly as Jes instructed. And Jes watched it all, his chest heavy with anticipation.

"Just like that," Jes whispered.

Moros chuckled quietly, pulling his body against Jes's.

This God.

Jes snapped himself from his thoughts, holding his head high. He could do this. There was nothing special about Moros. Nothing that should make him so weak in his knees. He was just a Governing God after all.

"Hold on tight," Jes said quietly, wrapping his arms around Moros's lower back.

Moros let out a gasp, pulling a responding grin from Jes's lips.

Jes stared ahead, refusing to allow the aching need coursing through him to distract him further. His shoulders rolled with the muscles of his wings taking control, pulling them from their relaxed stance behind him, upward and fanning out. Closing his eyes, he called to the wind, bringing it toward him like all the times he had before.

The wind rushed around him, picking up the soft powder of snow at his feet. Moros gasped quietly, the heat of his breath tickling Jes's neck. Shivering, Jes kept his eyes closed, his fingers moved along the wind, calling to it, commanding it.

When he was ready, the breeze caught the edges of his wings, bringing them toward the sky.

"I hope you're holding on," Jes whispered, launching up into the air before Moros could reply.

The usually arrogant God let out a scream that ignited Jes's blood and finally, the Beskermer allowed his eyes to open. His chest grew heavy while he wondered if he would get lost in the blue that stared back at him. Moros held his gaze never once blinking as Jes's wind guided them upward, taking control while Jes was sure he was slipping away from reality.

His hands tightened around Moros, and he glanced down, not realizing he'd wrapped his arms around his waist. But now that they were in the air, he didn't care. Because when he flew, he was weightless, bondless—he was Jesiel and only Jesiel. And having the silk of Moros's dark hair brushing against the tops of his hands, with the chill of Veturs around them, Jes had never felt so free.

"Beautiful," Moros muttered, still not pulling his eyes away.

Ripping himself from his mesmerism, Jes cleared his throat, focusing on his aching muscles begging to take control from the wind around them. Jes held Moros tighter, placing himself back into his role of protector. He couldn't drop a Governing God, even if that God had taunted him with this flight.

"Where did you want to go?" Jes asked, glancing down at Moros's grin.

Moros winked before tilting his head backward. "I'm afraid if I let go that I'll be dropped to the ground, but if you go straight toward that mountain, you're heading in the right direction."

Jes smirked at the fear shaking Moros's voice as he spoke. This God was scared but oddly trusting of a Beskermer that wasn't his own. Pulling his head upward, Jes spotted the mountain in the distance and picked up his speed, allowing his muscles to guide his wings.

Moros's grip around his neck grew tighter, his body pressing against Jes's for comfort. Jes kept his eyes forward, holding Moros as closely as he could without opening his mind to the taunting daydreams begging for their chance to play.

The wind stayed at their side while he flew, guiding them when his wings needed a break. The quiet friend that Jes had always run to when his thoughts were too much for him to be alone with. Providing that silence he needed when his mind couldn't do it for him.

The air around them shifted and Jes glanced up after the first flake of snow slid down his forehead. Creating a wet trail in its wake. His eyes narrowed and he snapped his gaze to where Moros hung to him.

"Stop that," Jes demanded.

Moros grinned, the fear in his eyes fading for a moment. "I thought you liked my season?"

Jes stiffened, his hands on Moros's back gripping the God's shirt. "Your mountain is just up ahead, where am I going next?"

Moros tilted his head back, his hair hanging in waves. "Go over the ridge and you'll see a small alcove with a jut of rock sticking off the end. Land there."

Jes grunted, pulling Moros closer to him. Moros let out a gasp at the movement, his fingers gripping Jes's neck.

"Stop that," Jes snapped while he maneuvered over the ridge.

Moros laughed, the air somehow growing cloudier with the sound. "You might as well admit when you like something, Jesiel. It's only you and me up here."

Jes shook his head, refusing to be distracted by Moros's teasing. Spotting the alcove, Jes began his descent. The wind followed behind him, guiding his wings and body down until they landed softly on the white powder covering the ledge.

Jes stared into Moros's eyes, realizing the God was now standing on his toes. But the weight of him was nothing compared to the heat between their bodies. The unbearable pull of him tugged at Jes to move closer, to pull Moros's body against his own. To allow the sudden heavy snow fall to lay over them like a protective blanket—hiding them from the world.

The snow below Jes's feet picked up with his wind, swirling around them while they held their gazes. As if his wind had heard his inner most thoughts, doing just as he wished, cloaking them in the whirlwind of a snow filled cyclone.

Moros's brow rose as his teeth bit his lower lip.

Jes's heart jumped. His eyes snapped from Moros's while he watched the man bite his lip again. The arms still wrapped around his neck pulled him closer until Jes's nose was brushing the tip of Moros's.

"What are you staring at, Beskermer?" Moros whispered.

Jes's chest grew heavy with his breaths. The wind around them grew stronger, blowing the silk of Moros's hair back in whimsical whisps.

"I—" Jes couldn't form the words. Not when the God kept biting his lip like that. Like a tease, an invitation to do the one thing Jes could never allow himself to have.

"Something catch your tongue?" Moros sneered.

The smirk on his face pulled Jes out of his trance and before he'd realized it, his hands were shoving Moros into the building snowbank behind them.

Moros let out a yell, his hands moving back to catch his fall. To Jes's surprise, the God didn't land on the ground. Instead, solid blue ice appeared below him, like a makeshift stool.

Moros landed on his ice with grace, his smiling growing wider.

"I'm older than you, Jesiel. I've got faster reflexes."

Jes didn't have time to react before a white sphere was barreling his way, colliding with the middle of his chest. His eyes widened and he let out a laugh, his head snapping to where Moros still sat casually on the ice block.

"Did you just throw a—"

His question was cut off when a smaller white ball hit him right in the face.

Wiping off the snow, Jes stared at Moros in shock. This Governing God had thrown a *snowball* at him. Not just one—two.

"Up for a challenge?" Moros teased, as his hands moved back and forth, and a third ball formed in his palms.

"You have the upper hand," Jes replied, bending and picking up as much snow as his palms could hold.

"Those *big* hands of yours have the upper hand," Moros replied, snapping his wrist and flinging the third ball Jes's direction.

Jes moved with ease, avoiding the freezing weapon to hit his body. Turning on his heel, he made eye contact with Moros, raising the snowball he'd formed.

"I suggest you run, Moros," he warned.

CHAPTER 8

Moros stared at the Beskermer, only allowing himself a moment to appreciate the beauty that was Jesiel Keita before he did as he was instructed—he ran. As fast as he could.

Holding back his shrieks, he ran past Jes, heading toward the other end of the alcove. Toward the hidden secret he'd intended to reveal.

The sound of Jes's wings fanning out behind him alerted Moros's senses and he picked up his pace, avoiding slipping on the ice in the alcove. He couldn't let this Beskermer best him, not in his own Region. Not when he truly had the upper hand.

"You may be older than me, Moros," Jes called out. "But that also means you're quite a bit slower than I am."

Moros laughed, throwing his head back before he collided with a solid wall of muscle. When he pulled his gaze upward, he offered Jes a mischievous grin.

"I suppose we couldn't call a truce?" Moros asked.

Jes said nothing, only offering Moros his own wickedly tempting grin before the ball of snow in his palm was suddenly colliding into the side of Moros's head.

Moros gasped from the shock of the cold while his body ignited with a rush of thrill and excitement. This winged beast wanted to play, and oh how he was willing to oblige. Throwing out his hand, Moros called to the cold, beckoning his beloved freeze to take control.

The ice flew from his palm, covering the floor of the hidden alcove in brilliant frigid blue. Jesiel yelped behind him and Moros bit back his responding laugh. Holding his shoulders high, he rushed to the back of the alcove, not willing to tell the Beskermer of his secret.

"Get back here!" Jesiel yelled behind him. Followed by a loud grunt and the crash of his massive body slipping on the ice.

Moros laughed then, shaking his head. "You have to catch me, Beskermer!" he yelled out.

Expertly, Moros moved deeper into the alcove, allowing his memories and senses to guide him as the light dimmed around him. Even after decades of retreating to his private escape, he had never gotten used to the few moments of complete darkness. But he kept going, ducking as the ceiling lowered above him, enclosing him in the tunnel he now headed down.

Jes's loud grunts provided him constant entertainment while the Beskermer fumbled his way behind Moros. Admirable really, when Jes had no idea where Moros was leading him. Making the beastly man even more intriguing.

"How are the wings?" Moros yelled out tauntingly.

"Fuck off," Jes grunted behind him.

Moros grinned with triumph. Focusing on his steps and allowing Jes's echoing sounds of annoyance to fade behind him, Moros continued down the dark tunnel. Soon the darkness surrounding him began to lighten, a reprieve from the suffocating bleakness they'd been traveling down.

"Where are you leading me?" Jes asked, causing Moros to jump from how close the Beskermer had gotten.

"I'm simply going on an adventure. You're the one who chose to follow."

Nerves filtered through Moros as the light grew brighter. He'd never brought anyone to his private escape. He wasn't even sure if his father had known this place existed in his large Region. Not when the man had been so focused on ruling the Region, and his son, with cruelty.

With his hands balled at his side, Moros called to the powers that chilled his blood and bones. It was the cold he retreated to when he was lost in the torment of his mind but he startled when a large warm palm landed on his shoulder.

"Moros?" Jes's voice was but a whisper in the wind.

Moros shook off the touch, stepping forward once more. Something had pushed him to show this giant beside him his most sacred place. And he could only hope the Beskermer wouldn't do anything to make Moros regret that choice.

"Pay attention, Jesiel," Moros said quietly.

Jes was silent behind him, but the warmth at his back was a tether tugging at Moros's soul.

The ceiling grew tall with the growing light and Moros straightened as he approached the wall of ice before him. The wall hadn't always been there. No, when he was but an adolescent, Moros had created that wall with his own hands. Expertly crafting the ice to protect that place his heart had led him to.

The wind picked up while Moros waved his hand across the blue wall before him. The landscape of his secret shimmered in the background. His wall shuddered beneath his palm but the fear in his heart hammered in protest. Begging him to turn back. To keep this place hidden from the world.

Moros glanced back, finding Jes's glistening golden eyes staring at him. Jes offered him a reassuring nod, placing one finger over his full lips. The silent agreement that he understood Moros was about to show him something secret.

With a deep exhale, Moros laid his palm flat against the ice and his beautiful blue wall fractured.

The sound echoed down the tunnel behind them, filling the small room they stood in with loud cracks. But no ice came their direction. There was no destruction or injuries.

Because this was *his* ice, and it obeyed his command.

Moros stepped back, watching the wall shift and fracture further. The once solid structure began to flow in blue rushing waves.

A waterfall of freezing water. Fit for a God of Wintur.

His breath caught in his chest while he admired his work. He smiled briefly at the loud sounds of Jes's breathing next to him. Like he'd stolen the Beskermer's ability to speak.

"Follow me," Moros whispered, gripping Jes's hand and pulling him toward the water.

Jes let out a loud gasp in surprise, but Moros laughed back. This water—his water—wouldn't soak them. It parted like a simple curtain, welcoming Moros back home.

He stood with his cold hand in Jes's, watching him study the landscape. Watching those golden eyes take in his surroundings. Slowly the scowl on Jes's face softened and his eyes shifted from frantic observation to slow appreciation.

Moros pulled his gaze from Jes, turning to admire his most beloved place. His eyes traveled around the small tree-line valley before him. The snow falling around them in a quiet welcome. Never in the years that he'd visited had the snow stopped falling. Even on cloudless days, like some spell had been placed on it. Never allowing the area to forget what Region it belonged to.

Pulling Jes with him, Moros walked down the long spiraling walkway that led to the small valley floor, where a frozen lake shimmered in the snow and sun.

Jes was silent throughout it all. His hand flexing in Moros's palm. But he didn't let go. Not once. As though Moros had stuck him in a trance.

When they reached the bottom of the path, Moros released Jes's hand. His eyes traveled to Jes's gaze finding tears lining the large man's eyes.

"I've always loved the snow," Jes whispered.

Moros kept his eyes on Jes as he moved his hands along the wind. The freeze effortlessly sprang from his fingertips, covering the bottoms of their shoes with solid ice.

"What are you doing?" Jes exclaimed, stumbling backward.

Moros stood, confidently balancing on his feet, amused by the fumbling limbs of the usually stoic man before him. "Bare shoes are not allowed on my ice, Beskermer. We have to glide to get over there."

His finger pointed to the small cabin hidden between two large, snow-covered pines trees. Its chimney smokeless begging to be lit. Waiting for bodies to warm its empty space.

"I don't..." Jes's uncertainty trailed off as he ran his hand over his short, cropped hair.

Moros laughed, the sound echoing out across the small valley floor. "Hold my hand, you winged beast and let me lead the way."

Jes's palm engulfed his own, and he nodded silently in agreement. The sliver of trust ignited a fire in Moros's soul.

With ease, Moros stepped forward, the ice now fused to his thin shoes gliding across the ice of the lake. The solid surface groaned beneath his initial movements. Jostling the lake awake from months of isolation since his last visit.

With a squeeze of Jes's palm, Moros gave him a reassuring smile and together they took off. Moros moved across the lake, the cut of his ice-blade filling his ears with beautiful precision. His hair flew back behind him, taking a weight of worry from him in an instant.

He brought Jesiel along with him, his silent companion whose feet stumbled and tripped over themselves. Inspiring a deliciously evil idea in Moros's head.

Moros released their grasp and skated away, expertly moving on the ice, moving his feet back-and-forth in waves while he watched Jes's eyes widened in fear.

"Get back here!" Jes begged as his hands reached forward desperately.

Moros only shook his head, offering Jes a wink as he glanced back at the cabin he approached. "Come and get me, Jesiel!"

Jes's wings fanned back behind him, but Moros stopped, holding himself still on the ice below him. "No cheating, Jesiel. Listen to the wind, feel the ice working together. *Come to me.*"

The last sentence left his lips like a taunt. The words lingered in the air while the snow seemingly paused its falling around them. Moros's world and Region waiting with bated breath to see what the mysterious Beskermer would do. To see whether or not he would accept the challenge.

Jes's awkward fumbling paused, and his eyes held Moros's gaze. Causing the God of Wintur's knees to weaken. If only momentarily.

Then the ice groaned, and Moros watched the giant man move. A picture of grace. Of strength. The perfect image of a Beskermer's power and duty. Heading right toward him with the most care-free grin splayed across his face.

Joy—freedom—everything this hidden valley brought to Moros's own heart.

Moros whipped around, lowering himself slightly, angling his arms to pump and propel him across the ice. The wooden cabin sat in the distance, his target and the goal. The sound of Jes gaining on him across the frozen lake, lingered in the air while Moros flew himself forward. He didn't have to speak to understand; the first one to the cabin was the winner.

The falling snow resumed, coating the lake with dangerous dust but Moros kept moving forward. The building was so close now he was sure if he reached out he'd touch its rough walls.

Then a flash of feathers brushed past the corner of his sight and Moros glanced upward, finding Jesiel before him. Mimicking the effortless back and forth swiveling of his feet Moros had been doing moments before their race.

"How did you figure that out?" Moros asked in amazement.

Jes smiled back, his arms crossed over his broad chest. "I'm a Beskermer. I've been taught to pay attention, learn, adapt, and succeed my entire life."

Moros's competitive nature danced inside of him. It pressed to be let out, to push forward and win this silly race. But watching Jes move so gracefully across the ice—watching the scowl on his face soften and his wings relax—it was the only victory Moros needed.

They were both silent for the few remaining moments it took to reach the other end of the lake. Letting out a content sigh, Moros lifted his foot and the ice at the bottom on his show shifted to soft puffs of snow, flying away with the wind.

His wrist flicked slightly, sending the ice on Jes's shoes away as well before he walked up the slight incline to the front door of the cabin.

With a hand wrapped around the icicle doorknob, Moros turned back to Jes. "This cabin is warded to warm instantly at my touch." He paused for a moment, his palm trembling against the ice. "And I've never shown anyone this hideaway before."

Jes nodded. "This secret is safe with me."

Letting out a breath, Moros returned a nod before pushing the door open. A rush of warm air shot out with the wind taking it out into the sky and Moros's eyes laid on the blazing hearth in the center of the room.

Slowly, he walked forward, motioning for Jes to follow him. But he kept his eyes on the fire. Not glancing back at his quiet companion. Then the door clicked shut and Moros forced himself to turn on his heel.

Jes's eyes were observing the single-room building. Landing on the large chair in the corner. Then the piles of furs and blankets in the middle of the room where a small stack of pillows sat at the top.

His body stiffened and Moros let out a laugh.

"The furs are faux. No animals were harmed in the warming of my home."

Jes grunted then glanced back at his wings Moros realized were now standing at attention. Moros threw his hair over his shoulder before laughing once more. "Jesiel, I know Beskermers frown upon animal hide in any manner. Riki has educated me on that matter."

"Not every *God* cares even if their Beskermers have told them," Jes replied harshly.

Moros rolled his eyes. "I don't care what other *Gods* do. I'm not one of them."

Jes was silent while the usual scowl he held on his face returned. Huffing out an annoyed breath, Moros lowered to the ground, patting the plush covers beneath him. Reluctantly, Jes followed the request, lowering himself beside Moros, who grinned back in triumph, leaning back on his hands.

"Tell me something about yourself, Jesiel." Moros cooed.

"Like what?" Jes replied, annoyed.

"Like why you hate yourself," Moros replied.

Jes stared in shock—shocked the God had so expertly seen through his life-long mask.

CHAPTER 9

Moros smiled back at Jesiel, celebrating that he'd hit his mark. He'd shocked the Beskermer with his observation, taking away the brute's ability to reply.

"Well?" Moros pried.

Jes shook his head. "I don't know what you're talking about."

Moros laughed, laying back against the furs beneath him. "You are such a bad liar, Beskermer. I see it in your eyes every time you admire my body. I see it in how rigid your shoulders become when my skin touches yours. You hate that you're attracted to me."

Jes jumped to his feet. The weight of his large body landing on the ground shook the cabin.

"Stop it," he demanded.

Moros stared up at him in shock, unsure how to respond to such a show of upset.

"Calm down," he said coldly. "I was just making an observation."

"Well, stop," Jes replied.

"You followed me here because I admitted something to you," Moros said, shifting his eyes to the dark wood ceiling above.

Jes grunted above him. "You apparently can't stop thinking about me."

"Yes, Jesiel. I can't stop thinking about you." Moros smiled at the brute. "Now admit you're attracted to *me*."

Jesiel stared at him blankly, but Moros held that gaze. Observing all that lingered in the frantic gold that held his attention. The fear, almost amusing when the beast that was Jesiel Keita usually appeared fearless.

"Stop playing games," Jes finally replied.

Moros's smile dropped from his lips.

Getting the Beskermer to admit what was still a locked-up piece of himself would prove more challenging than he had thought. Moros laid back on the blankets, placing his hands across his chest and intertwining his fingers.

He considered his plans—to get close to this terrified, towering coward—and wondered if it would be useless.

When Jesiel appeared to be stuck in the cycle of fear.

One Moros had left behind him decades before.

The cabin grew quiet with only the cracking of the fire filling the room. Making Moros wonder how long they'd sit in silence avoiding each other's eyes. Perhaps that's what they both needed though—silence.

In a world where they were both duty bound in their own way, he wondered if either of them ever really enjoyed complete silence.

He was lost in his thoughts and jumped when Jes sat beside him once more. His large palm barely a fingers-length away from where Moros's hand had relaxed against the blankets and furs.

Moros glanced at him, holding back his grin.

Jes was staring out the large window overlooking the frozen lake, and while he appeared rigid and uncomfortable, Moros noted the wings. How they slowly relaxed and the tips of them lazily brushed the floors of the cabin.

"I—" Jes started then paused.

Moros sat up, meeting Jes's eyes. "Yes?"

Jes offered a tempting shy grin that sent shivers down Moros's spine.

"I am attracted to you," he muttered, casting his eyes to the furs beneath him.

Moros grinned a triumphant grin. "Was that so hard to admit?"

"You're lucky to live a life so carefree in who you are. In what and who you want. That's a privilege, Moros. One you take for granted."

Moros didn't expect the immediate rage that boiled inside of him. His hands balled around the blanket beneath him.

"You have no idea what you're talking about," he snapped back.

His hair swung against his back when he turned his head back to glare at Jes. Where he found the Beskermer with a shocked expression across his face.

"Then tell me," Jes replied.

"A truth for a truth?" Moros countered.

Jes's eyes widened, and his wings shot back up to the stiff position he always held them in.

Moros rolled his eyes.

"It's only fair, Jes. Our own little *deal.*"

Jes nodded once, not uttering a sound. His hand rose as though motioning for Moros to speak.

Moros gulped, fear raising in his chest. He rarely—if ever—spoke about his own pain in his youth and adolescence. Even Riki had to pry information from him, and she was usually only successful when he'd consumed enough wine to loosen his lips.

"My father was a bastard," Moros forced himself to say. He turned his head from Jes, focusing on the snowstorm beginning to fall over the valley.

The thick flakes, unique and each their own, all responded to the fear in his heart. His magic trying to layer the earth with the cold he was most comfortable with.

Moros took a breath, pushing himself to continue.

"He kept himself tucked away usually. Rarely venturing out in public, at least any public outside of his Region. But he kept a firm hand over his citizens. A tyrant in his own way."

The room began to feel too warm with the snow growing thicker outside. Suddenly, Moros was on his feet, heading right for the front door.

He flung it open, breathing in the comforting scent of the cold mingled with the burning wood from the chimney.

Slowly, he sank to the floor, resting his back against the open door while his hands traced the dusts of snow coating the porch.

"My mother may have been the child of a King and the sister of the next King. She may be the first Goddess of Wisdom in only the Fates know how long, but that didn't mean she had full control over *him*. Especially not in how he attempted to raise me when I was under his roof."

Jes's heavy footsteps creaking against the cabin floor pulled Moros from his snow. He glanced up, finding Jes pointing to the spot beside him. Still unspeaking, but an understanding shimmer glistened in his eyes.

Moros nodded, allowing the company while he finished his admission.

"He was ashamed of me, Jesiel. Ashamed of my carefree nature. Ashamed that I preferred men over women. I was *the dark spot amongst his brilliant pure white*, as he liked to remind me."

Moros couldn't find any additional words to admit. Because the few he'd said had taken the breath from his chest. Pulling away the feigned confidence he held each day.

Sending him right back to a young boy standing in an ice palace, begging the Fates for his father to love him. Every part of him.

Jes palm wrapped around Moros's hand and Moros's head snapped up.

"What are you doing?" he demanded.

The Beskermer still said nothing, only squeezing Moros's hand softly.

Moros stared down at their clasped hands, his heart swelling. There was something magical about their touch together. How Jes's warmth somehow did not fully take his own cold. As though there was some unseen barrier between the two of them forcing their bodies to work together.

"I wonder if our Fathers could have been brothers," Jesiel said quietly.

Moros's mouth opened in shock, not expecting Jesiel to have uttered a word.

Jes leaned back against the door, pulling Moros's hand to his chest.

"He trained shame into me. Every single day. It was always under a pretense of duty and a *Beskermer's* purpose. But every day was not only a physical beating, *done for my own good,* but a verbal one as well."

Moros leaned his head against the door, turning it to meet Jes's gaze.

Jes smiled back at him, holding his hand tighter.

"It was always public too. These loud proclamations of what myself and my peers were expected to achieve. And even with it being public, I knew he was addressing only me—the son he was ashamed to call his own."

Jes released Moros's hand while he pushed away from the door.

"Then he died."

Moros kept his mouth shut. He remembered the scandal of Jes's father's passing. Most importantly how the King had released the Beskermer from their Fated bond just days before.

"Isn't it ironic that the duty he was so sure would guide his life's purpose was the same duty that ended it?"

Moros's eyes widened. The words leaving Jes's lips were masked with accusation. Words of treason. Words Moros knew would send his uncle into a rage if the Beskermer uttered them aloud.

"Jes—" Moros warned.

"I know," Jes replied, shaking his head. "I can't speak my assumptions. I can't voice how in the Fates a man as old as my father, nearly one thousand years walking this earth, was so easily felled. I can't voice that only his duty—the bond he'd been forced to renounce—led to his destruction."

Jes turned his head again, offering Moros a sad smile. "Sometimes I wonder if perhaps my own duty will do the same to me. If one day the path I've been following so loyally will lead to me losing everything that makes me—*me.*"

Silence settled over them again while they both turned their attention to the falling snow. Keeping their hands clasped, as though neither one were willing to release the comforting hold. To allow anything between them and the small admissions they'd made.

Eventually, the sun rose, replacing the bright snow filled sky with a wintur glow.

But still, they didn't leave. Instead, they moved back to the middle of the room, sealing themselves away from the snow storm. Finding themselves pulling the furs and blankets over themselves while they watched the fire burn.

Moros nestled against Jes's chest. Jes's arms wrapped around him and Moros was sure he could stay in that moment forever. Hidden away and warm.

As warm as his cold body had ever been.

"Why does the fire never burn out?" Jes whispered, his chest rumbling against Moros's head.

Moros's hand lifted while he imagined his cold playing with the heat and flames.

"Warded flames. The fire starts the moment my foot hits the valley floor."

Jes's arms held Moros tighter while his voice whispered, "Impressive."

Moros glanced up, finding Jes's gaze lost in the flames. His heart swelled at the beauty and the orange dancing in the Beskermer's gold. Two colors creating their own show of the fire Moros now believed lived within the brute's soul.

His hand grasped Jes's again and he sighed.

"I agree. It's rather impressive."

CHAPTER 10

FIVE MONTHS AFTER CHALLENGE

Jes pulled his body upward, sweat running down his back while the gawking of his new recruits burned at his back. His wings flexed behind him, dragging against his body's attempt to finish his rep. To pull his heavy body upward and prove to those below him that they could and would become physically capable.

He focused on the strain in his biceps, the pull of the muscles growing stronger, and the distraction it provided his mind from wandering back to a snow-covered cabin in the woods.

Lost in his thoughts, he barely detected the gasps ringing out from across the camp. He dropped from the bar he'd gripped, turning on his heel to find Roan stalking through the camp. With his black Pegasus, Nacht, trailing closely behind him.

Jes's brow crumpled. In the five months since he'd taken over the Guard from Nas, Aeron's Beskermer, Roan hadn't visited. Shifting on his feet, Jes watched Roan approach and every head around him dip into a bow.

Roan gave Jes an amused smile, but Jes only rolled his eyes. He was irritated that Roan was encroaching on his space, his domain in this Region he'd been forcefully assigned to.

Roan's smile dropped, likely from the scowl on his Beskermer's face. When he was finally before Jes, he snapped his fingers, allowing the recruits and guards to rise from their bows.

"My Pegasus needs water," Roan pointed to the recruits gathered beside Jes. "Please take this as a group training lesson and make sure the future Pegasus of Death isn't injured."

Whispers filled the air of the training camp, but no one moved. Scowling at Roan further, Jes turned on his heel, raising his voice. "You all heard your Governing God. Get our asses moving. Now!"

Dirt kicked up with their scrambling and the small group gathered around Nacht, who amusingly, took off across the camp.

"Well," Jes yelled. "Go catch the fucking animal!"

The recruits all yelped, and their limbs flailed as they ran off after Roan's Pegasus.

Now alone together, Jes turned to his friend. "You planned that."

Roan laughed, slapping his hand against Jes's back. "Fates, that Pegasus is going to run them ragged."

"They're adults, Roan. Not children," Jes replied, brushing away Roan's hand.

Roan's demeanor dropped and he nodded. "Barely adults. Let's not forget that."

"Is there something you need from me?" Jes questioned, motioning for them to sit on a bench near Jes's office at the camp.

Roan nodded his head, pulling a white scroll from his pant pocket. "My aunt has requested some assistance with record keeping in Moudrost. She acknowledges I can't attend due to having just acquired the Region and requests your presence instead."

Jes froze, his hands now trembling in his lap. "Moudrost?" he asked.

Roan stared back, his head cocking. "Yes... Is that an issue?"

"What does she mean by *record keeping*?"

Jes stared out at the training camp, imagining the trip to the Region of Wisdom. Where the Goddess, Roan's aunt, resided.

The mother of the God Jes had been trying to rid his mind of since that evening wrapped in furs in a secret cabin nestled in a hidden valley in the mountains.

Roan shuffled beside him. "She needs to ask questions regarding the challenge, events that took place afterward, and what the scholars can expect from the new God of Nyte."

"Has she made this request of your brother?" Jes asked.

Roan nodded. "Arno is going in his place."

Jes groaned. "A forced family reunion."

"Amada has confirmed she's scheduled you to arrive days after your cousin. It'll just be you there."

Jes stood, wiping his pant leg. "Why can't the scholars come here?"

Something about this odd request had a certain God of Wintur's hand all over it. Jes could feel it, almost to his bones, that Moros was part of this.

Roan stared back at him blankly. "I'm actually not sure." He stood, offering the scroll to Moros. "I could challenge it, but—"

"You don't want to come across as difficult in your new position," Jes completed the sentence.

He reached forward, gripping the scroll when ice cold zapped at his palm. He yelled out, dropping the scroll into the dirt.

"What in the Fates was that?" Roan exclaimed beside him.

Jes shook his head, staring at the scroll on the ground. He held up his hand, preventing Roan from approaching it. "I overdid it with trying to show my strength to the recruits," he lied. "I'm fine."

Slowly, Jes bent, picking up the scroll. The cold zapped him again but not enough to shock him.

Straightening, Jes squared his shoulders. He glanced at Roan and nodded his head. "I'll fulfill your Aunt's request."

Roan tilted his chin. "Thank you. Jes—" Roan stepped forward, an obvious need to discuss the current rift between the two of them, but Jes stepped back.

"I'm your Beskermer. I fulfill my duties, Roan. For now, can we leave it to that?"

Roan nodded again as his hand ran through his hair. "Please let me know if there is any information you're unable to provide the scholars and I will address them directly with Amada."

Jes's grip on the parchment tightened while Roan walked away.

Once his Governing God had reached the group of recruits still attempting to catch the Pegasus, Jes unrolled the scroll, his heart hammering in his chest. His eyes narrowed while the parchment grew colder and the note, previously appearing to have been written by the Goddess of Wisdom, shifted to lettering written by a different hand.

Jesiel,
You've received my note. Isn't it so much fun to deceive every-
one?
Meet me in Moudrost. Let's make some history together.
What do you say?
—Moros

Jes rolled the parchment back up, his eye catching the shimmering black wings of Roan's Pegasus catching flight. He glanced around the camp, his duty, another symbol of his loyalty and he smiled.

He carefully placed the parchment in his pocket as his wings fanned out behind him, lifting him toward what was bound to be an adventure.

With his pack on his shoulder, Jes made his way through the cobbled streets of Kennis, holding his head down. He hadn't been sure Amada wasn't actually expecting him and as a Beskermer, he stood out amongst the grey-robed scholars that littered the main city of Moudrost.

He kept his wings tucked in tight as he headed toward the direction Moros had left further down in his deceptive letter. The brickstone buildings lining the streets of Kennis wrapped in an upward spiral as Jes trekked up the streets.

Warm light shone through the windows but other than the robed scholars, no citizens were out on the blisteringly warm evening. Jes shivered, it was eerie being in a main city so empty. And this city—it was as though the very streets themselves whispered the secrets kept in the libraries on every corner.

Reaching the top of the hill, Jes stopped in his tracks when he laid eyes on the building before him. He cursed under his breath, not realizing he'd been fooled by the God again.

Moros had sent him right to the doorstep of the Palace of Wisdom.

The center of attention in this knowledge ridden Region.

Letting out an annoyed huff, Jes turned on his heel, ready to head back to the city's Perambulate when an icy hand gripped his wrist.

Moros pulled Jes back to him, a smile bright on his lips. "Hello," he chimed.

Jes yanked his arm away, tucking it against his body. "The palace, Moros? Really? Do you intend to embarrass me publicly?"

Moros's smile dipped before his regular unphased expression returned. "I'll have you know, Jesiel," he paused, motioning his finger for Jes to follow him, "my mother is actually expecting you. I only skewed the dates a little."

"When is she expecting me?" Jes replied, shuffling to keep up with the God.

"Tomorrow. That means I have an *entire* day with you to myself."

Jes huffed. "What if she sees me?"

"Then we tell her that Roan sent you early. Why are you so flustered, Beskermer? Were you expecting to receive something that's now off the table?"

Moros whipped around, winking before his hands pushed open the carved oak doors they'd approached.

Jes shook his head, irritated by his amusement at the God's games. His hands ran over the oak as they crossed the threshold, his heart tightening at his natural response to the wood.

The sound of tree branches swaying in the wind filled his memories. The smell of fires late at night. The creak of bridges high in the sky connecting treetop houses.

"Jesiel?" Moros's quiet voice pulled Jes from his thoughts and he stared back at the God.

"Yes?"

Moros glanced over nervously and Jes followed his gaze, finding his cousin beside the Governing Goddess of Wisdom. Both of them staring at Jes with their mouths open.

Jes's eyes widened as he made eye contact with the Goddess. Quickly, he dropped his sack and dipped into a bow. Showing his respect to the Goddess gracefully opening her Region to him.

"Stand, Beskermer," Amada's voice rang out.

Jes straightened, picking up his pack while catching the smirk across his cousin's lips.

"Arno," he said curtly.

"Cousin," Arno replied. "I thought our visits were not supposed to overlap one another's?"

Amada's eyes traveled beyond Jes's head where a silent Governing God of Wintur sat. Her arms crossed over themselves before her gaze softened. "Did my nephew misunderstand my note?"

Jes held his composure, fighting back the urge to hit the smirk off his cousin's face. "No, my Lady. I believe I may have misunderstood." He shook his head. "Roan is quite busy in his new role, and he is regularly in Shadus with Aeron receiving guidance on how Nacht has been ruled for the last Millennia. Your messenger passed the note directly to me."

Amada's brow crumpled before she lifted her hand. "As such, I cannot begin with you until I have addressed my questions with the God of Daee's Beskermer." Her fingers snapped and she waved her son forward. "Moros, please show Jesiel to one of the guest rooms." Her eyes glanced at Arno before she continued. "I think it's best if he's placed in the *west* wing of the palace."

"Yes, mother," Moros replied.

Jes offered the Goddess a respectful nod then turned to follow Moros's retreating footsteps.

"What game are you fucking playing?" Jes growled, grabbing Moros's arm once they had disappeared from the Goddess's view.

"Shut up, Beskermer and follow me," Moros replied.

Jes froze, watching as Moros turned down a hall with book-lined walls.

He blinked. He'd heard the stories of the Palace of Wisdom. How the halls themselves were built by the stories of their worlds. Of their history.

He just hadn't thought it was literal.

"Are you coming?" Moros called over his shoulder.

Jes grumbled, picking up his pace as he followed the God down the winding halls. His wings twitched behind him while he attempted to keep them tucked in tight, avoiding the likely priceless history he was passing with each step.

His ears rang at the buzz in the ear. Just like out on the street. This Region and its ability to collect history and knowledge from the moment your foot stepped foot on its soil.

Jes shivered. The secrets this palace must hold.

Now I'm holding my own secrets.

Moros stopped before him, holding open a narrow door. Jes scowled, dipping down and finding himself back in the foyer of the palace.

"What?"

He twisted around finding the Goddess and his cousin gone.

"Thank the Fates," Moros whispered. "Now we can continue on with my plan."

Jes gawked at Moros, rage building inside of him.

"What games are you playing, Moros?" he exclaimed.

"We've got to leave now if I want to get you back by tomorrow," Moros replied.

"Where are we leaving to?" Jes demanded, his eyes surveying the vast foyer.

Moros pointed and Jes turned, finding the tapestry Moros pointed to. Only, his eyes caught the golden shimmer behind the tapestry.

"My mother's portal is located in a rather public location. But it's better than the Perambulate."

"Where are we going?" Jes repeated.

"To Veturs of course," Moros grinned. "Or would you prefer alone time in my mother's house? I won't shame your preferences."

Jes's eyes widened. "I'm not here to give you whatever you're hoping for."

Moros approached; the cold of his magic crawled up Jes's body. His fingertips brushed Jes's skin, and he leaned forward, his lips brushing Jes's ear.

"Wouldn't you like to know what I'm hoping for?"

Jes stiffened, his heart racing as Moros walked away. His hands balled at his sides while he attempted to realign himself. Without his control, his hand lifted, brushing where the God's lips had touched his skin.

His mind went back to that cabin in the valley. Their hands clasped over each others. The heat of the fire. The desire that had coursed through him and how his cowardice had prevented him from going further.

Glancing back at the palace, Jes squared his shoulders and followed the God through the portal.

He nearly tripped on Moros's heel when they arrived back in Veturs, the immediate cold calling out to Jes once more.

Jes held onto his pack while he observed the room. It was very much Moros with the glass table, an ice seat, and a fire ironically not melting a single frozen surface.

"You've brought me to Veturs," Jes stated. "What now?"

Moros grinned. "Dinner, Jes, and then bed."

Jes shook his head. "I'm not here to warm your bed, Moros."

"Dinner then," Moros replied, clapping his hands.

Jes's pack dropped to the ground as a small glass table topped with steaming food appeared before them.

"Fates, I love wards." Moros laughed. "Speaking of, did you like my letter?"

Jes avoided Moros's outstretched hand while he settled into one of the empty chairs. "That was impressive, I will admit that. Where did you learn it? That would be very helpful in my Beskermer duties."

Moros shrugged. "Being the child of the Goddess of Wisdom has its perks. One is being surrounded by the oldest and most knowledgeable scholars in existence. My mother's most trusted confidant taught me how to write hidden messages when I was an adolescent."

Jes leaned back, studying Moros while he spoke. "Why?"

Moros's eyes glanced up from the red wine he poured into his glass. "My mother was not always welcoming to who I am. This scholar thought I needed a way to express myself without her judgement."

"Who did you write to?" Jes asked, accepting the glass Moros handed him.

Moros sipped from his cup. "Myself. In journals. You have to realize, Jesiel. I was the only child in my fucked-up family for over one-hundred years before Marek was born. Even worse, I've been the only one between myself and my cousins who has had Governing God duties for the last several decades. That can get rather lonely."

Jes nodded, pulling his glass to his lips. "What about Riki?"

"Riki is my Beskermer who runs this Region beautifully. It hasn't been until recent years that we've become friends. What you and Roan have is rare."

"I'm aware," Jes grumbled, irritated to be talking about the friend he was still upset with.

Moros leaned back. "I don't know what's going on between the two of you, but you shouldn't take that friendship for granted."

Jes set his glass on the table, running his hand over his short-cropped hair. "I don't. He's a brother to me. I will do anything to maintain the relationship that we have."

Moros's eyes narrowed behind the rim of his glass. "Beskermer loyalty is one to commend."

"What do you know about loyalty?" Jes shot back.

Moros startled then stood. "You wouldn't know, Jesiel. Because my *loyalty* prevents me from speaking about it."

Moros crossed the room, settling into a dark green armchair in the corner. "Tell me something, Jesiel. Tell me a secret about yourself. Something you've never told another soul."

Jes's fingers tapped against the table while he stared at the man. "Why?"

Moros's eyes softened. "Because I want to know you. Is that such a bad thing?"

"I'm not sure," Jes replied. "But I have to admit something."

"What is that?" Moros asked, his gaze turning away to glance at the hearth.

Jes moved while the God was distracted. His blood rushed to his ears as he found himself before the icy man. Kneeling, he tucked a piece of black hair behind Moros's ear.

Moros gasped and his hands shook on the arms of the chair. Jes grasped them, holding them to his lips.

"I want to know you as well," he whispered.

CHAPTER II

Jes's hands trembled against Moros's cheek as the words left his lips. His heart tugged at the way Moros's chest heaved up and down.

"I want to know you," Jes repeated.

His body jolted when Moros finally moved, leaning into his touch. The cold of his skin warmed against Jes's palm.

"You've broken into my mind," Jes whispered. "Every day is filled with cold. A tonic grasping my senses, preventing me from functioning."

Moros's eyes glistened as Jes continued.

"What have you done to me, you icy man?"

The admission left Jes's heart, and his body relaxed, perhaps for the first time in his life.

He stared into the shimmering blue eyes before him, his body rushing with emotions. Because there was nothing he wanted more than to know the God before him. All of him. Every piece that should have scared the trained Beskermer.

But as he beheld the beautiful man, Jes was more afraid to lose him.

Snow began to fall around them, hissing as it hit the heated stone of the hearth as they stared at each other. Neither man willing to move.

Jes's finger stroked Moros's cheek.

He was content. Perfectly happy to stay in that moment for the rest of his long life. Staring into the eyes and soul of possibly the only person who would never judge him.

Moros grunted and the sound pulled Jes from his thoughts.

"Yes?" Jes whispered.

Moros stared at him, his hand raising and Jes flinched. A grin crept across the God's face as his finger brushed Jes's lips.

"Kiss me, you brute," he muttered.

Jes's hand moved down, gripping the collar of Moros's shirt. He pulled the God's face close to his, his lips barely moving as he replied.

"You want me to kiss you?"

Moros nodded, letting out a tiny gasp that sent shivers down Jes's spine. Then he obliged, pulling the God toward him and colliding his lips into addicting cold.

Moros's arms wrapped around Jes's neck while their lips moved against each other's. Every ounce of control Jes had over himself cracked. Opening the cage he kept locked up, washing over the trained years of hating himself.

He pressed himself against Moros, wrapping his hands in the silky, long hair. Pressing his hips against Moros's, soaking in the firm chest against his own.

His arousal strained against his trousers and he pulled at Moros's lower lips when the God's own firm response pressed against his own.

Then the cold against his lips was gone and Moros was pulling away.

Jes stumbled, stepping back. "What?"

Moros's eyes scanned the study. "Not here."

"What?" Jes repeated, blinking through his arousal.

Moros's hand gripped his and he pulled him toward the doors.

For a moment, Jes wondered if he should follow. If he should risk being seen heading to wherever this God's bedroom lay in the palace. But as he stared at the long glistening locks of black hair before him, he rid himself of the thoughts.

Because he would go wherever Moros led him.

Even if that were into the very depths of Shadus themselves.

Silently they moved through the palace and Jes took note of the path. Committing to memory how to get to Moros's room.

They turned a corner, and before them was a long spiral staircase. Moros glanced back at him with a nervous grin.

"My room is solitary in this large palace. My place of sanctuary. I allow no one but myself in this spire."

Jes nodded in understanding. Moros was reassuring him. Giving him that thread of safety his tormented and conflicted mind needed.

"Take me to your bed, Moros," Jes replied, dropping his voice.

Moros smiled again and together they climbed the staircase. Silently holding in both of their nerves while their hands stayed clasped tightly together.

Moros threw open the door and Jes stepped through, admiring the large fur-covered bed in the center. Another one of the God's warded fires ignited and Jes turned back to the man his heart yearned for.

Jes grasped Moros's hands and pulled him to the bed.

"I think I could love you," he whispered as he turned the God's body around and laid him gently against the mattress.

"Jes," Moros's voice cracked.

He was surprised by the words himself. Shocked at how quickly he was uttering them, but it was right. His soul knew it was right. Even if it were absolutely terrifying.

He leaned down, pressing his body against Moros's. Pressing the heat of their arousal together. Begging for a chance to lose themselves in each other.

Moros stared up at him and Jes was sure his heart would crack from the love in those blue eyes. A reflection of the icy God's soul.

Moros's hand rose, brushing against Jes's cheek. "I think I could love you too."

Jes leaned into the words, brushing his lips against Moros's.

"May I lay with you, Moros?" he whispered.

"By the Fates, you don't have to ask," Moros replied.

A soul defining silence filled the room while they carefully undressed each other. Both of their hands trembling while they removed the other's clothing. Like some sacred ceremony they were beginning. Possibly a life-time of this to look forward to.

Laying on the bed, Jes watched as Moros leaned over, pulling a small vile from his nightstand. The whole time, Jes was sure he was in a dream. Sure he would wake and find himself in his bed a Region over.

Alone.

Moros turned back, offering Jes a smile while he poured the oil into his palm.

"This is..." he began.

"I'm not inexperienced, Moros," Jes interrupted with a laugh. "I know exactly what that is."

Moros grinned, wrapping his hand around Jes's cock abruptly.

Jes bucked his hip, letting out a yell.

"I was going to say it's cold," Moros replied, tightening his grip around Jes.

Jes couldn't help but laugh in response. Because the words were lost while Moros worked his hands up and down his shaft. Pulling tension from his back and down his legs. Sending a need to release throughout his entire body.

Jes's hands gripped the bedspread while Moros's hand moved. He threw his head back, moving his hips occasionally with the soft but quick movements.

"Come here," he managed to choke out.

Moros stopped his hand and brushed his hair from his face. Then he moved and Jes drank him in. His eyes scanned the God's body. The firm muscles of his abdomen and arms. The dark skin, glistening from the oil and sweat from the unexplainable heat stifling the room.

As Moros moved, Jes reached out, wrapping his palm around his cock, providing his own strokes of pleasure.

Moros let out a groan as he fell beside Jes. His body shook and Jes moved his hand faster, lost in the captivating moans coming from the God's lips.

He leaned up on his free hand while he moved up and down Moros's shaft. Knowing the need to release that was building within the man he could not rid his mind from. Knowing the pleasure he was giving him.

Moros's head turned and he gave a struggled smile.

"Fates, that feels good," he muttered.

The sound of his voice breaking the silence filled Jes with need and he leaned forward, pressing his lips against Moros's.

Their kiss was madness—addicting. Distracting them both from touching each other while Moros leaned forward, pressing his chest against Jes's.

Jes laid back against the bed, shaking as Moros's firm cock pressed against his own. And then they pulsed against each other, sending frigid shocks down Jes's spine.

"I want you," Moros whispered against his lips.

"Then have me," Jes replied, wrapping his hands around Moros's abdomen and lifting the God. "Have me how ever you'd like, Moros," he said with a groan.

Moros leaned forward, picking up the vile of oil again and rubbing it into his palms. As he wrapped his hands around Jes again, Jes was sure he would lose himself too soon. Releasing before he was able to have the full moment he wanted with the man he loved.

Moros worked the oil up and down Jes's shaft, warming his skin with his cold touch.

A sensation Jes didn't understand how it was possible.

As Moros lowered himself onto Jes, his expression falling into pleasure and bliss, Jes bucked his hips in response from the heat of him wrapping around him.

The tightness with the slick of the oil collided with him all at once, forcing his body to beg to take control. To move until that tension was released from deep within him.

But he held back, gripping the blankets while Moros fully seated himself down.

"Touch me," Moros gasped rocking himself against Jes.

And Jes obeyed, wrapping his hand around Moros's rigid arousal, pulling up and down as Moros found his pace.

They kept their eyes on one another while Jes moved his palm up and down in tune with Moros's rising and falling body.

"Fates, Jes," Moros exclaimed when Jes swiped his finger over the bead of moisture slipping from his tip.

"More," Jes replied, lifting his hips and Moros upward.

His legs shook with the ecstasy of the movement and his hand gripped tighter.

"Jes," Moros cried out. His hands landing on his chest while he moved. But Jes didn't go. He wanted to bring as much pleasure to this man as he was bringing him. He wanted his release to cause his knees to weaken. He wanted him to lose his senses to the pleasure.

Silence settled around them again while their breaths blew out cold puffs of hot air as they moved together. Both determined to allow the other release.

Jes's body pulled tighter, an ache quickly building low.

"Moros," he groaned, moving his hand faster. "Moros, come with me."

Moros let out a quiet moan and he moved faster. Simultaneously pumping himself in Jes's palm as he moved up and down Jes's shaft.

Sweat ran down Jes's face while he moved faster, with more determination.

"Come with me," he repeated, dropping his voice to a command.

As the words left his lips ecstasy took over. His vision blurred and his hips moved upward as his release came. His free hand gripped Moros's thigh while his hand wrapped around him continued to move before warm liquid spilled from the God.

His eyes snapped down, watching Moros's release trail down his palm. A beautiful sight in itself.

Jes glanced around, searching for a towel.

"We didn't think that far ahead," Moros laughed.

Jes turned his gaze back to where Moros still sat a top him. Squeezing the thigh he still held, he laughed. "If I can borrow a shirt, we can use what I wore."

Moros smiled and nodded his head, as he stood quickly.

Together they cleaned up then settled back next to each other, pulling the thick comforter and furs around them.

Jes held Moros until his breathing slowed and he was sure his icy man had lost himself in whatever dreams his mind ran towards. Then silently, he slipped from the bed, regret in his heart that he was sneaking away.

Always running back to his duty.

Moros woke, finding the spot beside him cold. Tears built in his eyes while he scanned the room.

He thought something had changed. He thought Jes had accepted who and what he was. He thought it would be different after seeing every beautiful inch of that towering, muscular body.

But he'd been fooled.

CHAPTER 12

M oros stepped through his Governing God portal, right into the open foyer of the Palace of Wisdom. To no surprise, his mother was already waiting, standing stoically across the room. A look of both concern and disapproval tight across her face.

"Mother," Moros said quietly, dipping his head low in respect.

The Goddess of Wisdom said nothing while she crossed the foyer. She only held a mother's gaze, barreling into her son's tender heart.

Her palms wrapped around his and Moros's throat bobbed, noting the skin on her hands, slightly darker than the rest of her. The only subtle sign of the hours she spent each day flipping through the books and tomes that made up her brilliant Region. The mark of who she was. What knowledge she held. What secrets she knew.

"Moros," she whispered, brushing a sliver of his long hair behind his ear. "Why are you here?"

The question broke him. Cracking right through the hardened wall he was trying to build over his heart. Fracturing the miniscule remnants of strength he had.

"Mother," he whispered again, falling to his knees. Crashing against the marbled floor of the palace as the weight of everything fell over him in an instant.

His mother's comforting arms wrapped around him. The blanket of trust and safety he'd always run to in his life. The surety she would always be there. Always ready to provide the wisdom she ruled over.

"My son," she whispered. Offering quiet *shush*es while one hand stroked his hair.

After a few moments, she pulled away and Moros glanced up to find her arm outstretched. He took it, hesitantly, knowing the quiet request for a more private location.

Together they walked hand in hand down the book-lined halls of the palace of wisdom. The spines of each book watching their steps. And Moros was sure there was a whisper in the air. As though the pages themselves were filling with knowledge of the day. Quiet recounts of the history this Region so carefully collected and stored away for future generations to stumble upon.

His heart ached while he thought back on when he'd brought Jes here. The awe in those golden eyes. How they had scanned each spine that made up the walls. And how even then, Moros had felt it—the whispering. The quiet hushes of their secret trip being collected without their approval.

Their secret now locked away within the ever-knowing halls of Wisdom.

His tears lined while his mind wandered, and his feet mindlessly followed his mother through the home he'd grown up in. Finally, her steps slowed, her dress no longer swished against the wooden floors beneath them, and he looked up to find standing before her private study.

She gestured to the now open door, her motherly gaze gripping his aching heart.

"Come on," she whispered, offering him a soft smile.

Silently he crept into the study, placing himself on the encompassing armchair that sat in the corner of the quaint room. He watched while she muttered under her breath as her hands began tidying her small desk below the window. Just like he'd watched her so many times before in his life when she was too nervous to have a private conversation with him.

He blamed her fucked up family for the discomfort.

But she tried—always.

Even if it took her a while to build up the courage. She always found a way to put aside her own beliefs or opinions when he needed her most.

Finally, her nervous movements stopped and she approached, sitting down on the ottoman at the base of the chair he'd curled up on.

She patted the cushion at the tips of his toes, asking for his hand.

Moros took in a breath, tears lining his eyes while her palm wrapped around his.

"What's wrong?" she whispered.

"Mother," he choked. "I—" His words stuck in his throat while he stared off toward the small fire burning in the hearth behind her.

Ironic considering the heat of summer taking root over the world.

"Moros?" she asked again, prying him from his mind's attempt at distraction.

"I think I love him," Moros admitted, covering his face with his hands.

"Oh," his mother exclaimed, wrapping her arms around him. Cradling him close as the sobs tumbled from him. "Oh, my darling."

Moros laid his head against his mother's shoulder, the emotions taking him outside of his control. It was too much. Too fast. Too wrong.

Why?

Why was he so enamored by that beastly man? Why? When that same beast was so determined to keep him *secret*. To hide whatever this was between them from the world.

To hide *him*.

Moros hadn't been able to get past it. Not since that night together.

He'd thought he'd been taunting the Beskermer. Irritating him just enough that Jes would relent and convince Roan to listen to what he had to say. But too quickly that had changed.

It was the amusing irritation Jes held in his stance—constantly.

But it was also the smile, the laugh, the way the large man stared at Moros's beloved snow with the same wonder the God of Wintur felt in his heart.

A snowball fight.

A cabin sequestered in a secret valley.

Hands grasping one another before a fire.

Small moments together. Brief times of honesty—vulnerability.

All leading up to this...

Love.

When his tears finally dried, Moros pulled his head away from his Mother, staring into her knowing eyes.

He sniffled, dabbing his cheeks briefly. "I apologize," he muttered.

She laughed, the sound filling the small room. "I've seen you cry plenty of times in your life, my darling. This certainly won't be the last."

Slowly, she stood from the ottoman, making her way to her desk chair. Moros kept his eyes on her, watching her sink into her seat while her fingers tapped against the top of the desk.

"Why do you allow a *man* to cause you so much pain?"

Moros rolled his eyes. "You're one to talk."

Her eyes narrowed back, and he dipped his head down. "Sorry," he whispered.

"You're not wrong, I have let a man cause me pain before," she chuckled. "Fates, there were days in my youth when I thought he was my world. My savior."

Moros shifted uncomfortably. It was his own fault—bringing up his father and he instantly regretted his need to provide a snide comment. To appear stronger than whomever he spoke with.

You're just like him.

The thought rushed through his mind briefly and he pushed down his own self-disgust. He balled his hands in his lap and met his mother's eyes once more.

"As I was saying," she continued, acknowledging the few moments her son had been lost inside himself, "I let him destroy me for far too long, Moros. Even worse, I allowed him to destroy *you*." She stood, bracing against her desk and wrapping her arms around herself. "I just thought we had both found the strength to never allow that to happen again."

Moros shifted in his seat, turning his gaze from his mother. His eyes focused on the fire once more. The stifling heat bringing a sweat to his brow.

"I don't know how to fight this," he admitted.

The Goddess of Wisdom crossed the room once more, setting herself upon the ottoman. Her hands pressed against the wall under the window and a latch *clicked*, followed by a rush of summer air encircling them.

She let out a sigh, leaning back against her hands. "Do you *want* to fight it?"

"What?" Moros stared back in a daze. "You're beginning to confuse me, mother."

She gave him one of her teasing grins before glancing out the window. "My darling, as your mother I only want you to be happy." She leaned forward, resting her elbows on her knees. "You deserve happiness, Moros. You deserve love that is loud and open."

Her hands gripped his, pulling him out of his spiraling thoughts. "I know—" She made a choked sound, then shook her head. "I know I did not always handle who you are well."

Moros turned his head, finding tears in her eyes.

"Regret can be a mother's worst curse," she sniffled. "Regret for what we did or didn't do. How well we have or haven't reacted to our children being themselves."

Moros's throat bobbed with emotions. Her hands tightened around his while she continued.

"I can't ever take back the things I've done that have hurt you. And I never want you to believe I expect immediate forgiveness for them. I only know that my *son* deserves to be loved just as he is."

Her hand brushed his cheek. "You are special, Moros. I knew it from the first time your tiny, cold hand wrapped around my finger. If you believe you've found someone to compliment that special heart, then fine. But I will say it again, you deserve love that is paraded around our world, proudly boasting you are theirs and they are yours."

Moros allowed his tears to fall while he considered his mother's words. He'd come to her for her comfort, her grounding embrace, and annoyingly her wisdom. His lip trembled when he met her eyes again, his heart pounding against his chest.

"Does patience not have a place here? Does love not require patience?"

His mother cocked her head. "I suppose... but how long does one expect the other to be patient for? What sacrifices are expected to be made in the name of *love?*"

Moros nodded, letting her words settle over him.

His eyes cleared from the tears while he watched the grey-robbed scholars shuffle about the city below. He was surrounded by brilliant minds of wisdom and candor. Minds made for providing support and guidance. Yet, his heart rebelled against it all. Tugging at him to take his mother's portal to the Region of Nyte. To sneak through his cousin's door and slip into the bedroom beside the kitchen. Where a winged man would be waiting for him. Arms open and inviting, welcoming Moros into the bliss of his touch.

Moros leaned back, placing his hand over his chest.

But was the bliss enough? When he knew the heart between those outstretched arms was guarded and locked up. Possibly unwilling to open in the way Moros's heart had already begun to.

CHAPTER 13

Jes stared at the busy Perambulate building, studying each person who passed him. His hands shook at his sides while he contemplated his next step. Quickly, his head whipped back toward the manor on the hill, and he imagined Roan and Lahana on the lawn, staring at him.

Questioning where the Beskermer was going.

Except, Jes knew his mind only wished for him to imagine their judgement. Given they'd left the day before to Roan's summer cottage on the coast. Both of them mocking Jes's hate for the sand and sea as they went.

But like most summers, when Roan took his short vacation, Jes stayed behind.

Not to watch the Region or the guards at camp. No, it was usually his few days of quiet, alone time. When he'd find himself wandering around Iluna or flying off toward the mountains surrounding the small city.

Only this year...

His head turned back to the Perambulate and his heartbeat quickened.

He had somewhere—someone he could go to.

Nervously, Jes glanced at the bodies passing him and he wondered if any were taking note of the Governing God's Beskermer and Captain. As he stepped forward, not one head turned his way. The people surrounding him kept about their own business. Carrying their luggage for their own getaways or heading to occupations in other Regions.

Jes's wings fanned out behind him as he opened the doors of the Perambulate building, where the portal sat awaiting him.

For a moment he considered taking flight and going the long route to Moros. Letting the wind guide him high up in the sky while he considered what he would say to the God. But that gave him more time to back out. To turn around and head back to Iluna and hole up in his room. Hidden away until Roan and Lahana returned.

So, he queued up, keeping his head down until he was standing before the portal. Slowly, he approached the portal, reaching his hand through the shimmer calling to him. Stretching his fingers out to the unknown magic that controlled the portals they all traveled through.

His eyes closed while he pulled the wind around him, throwing his whisper out. Hoping the icy man on the other side could hear him.

Moros, will you see me?

Ice cold air wrapped around his body and Jes opened his eyes, watching in awe as frost came through the portal. Gasps rang out behind him, but Jes only grinned.

He stepped through, expecting to meet a smiling bright face. Instead, his feet hit the ice floors of the Palace of Wintur and he gazed upon a deep scowl across Moros's face.

Jes stared back, blinking with shock. Unsure of what he had done to possibly irritate the God already.

Moros said nothing, only letting out a *huff* and motioning for Jes to follow. Jes's head whipped around, trying to locate any staff whose prying eyes may be spying. But he found Moros's palace as empty as it usually was.

With an eerie chill whispering through the air while the God stormed off.

Picking up his pace, Jes rushed after, determined to learn what he'd done.

Or hadn't done.

Standing in Moros's study, Jes's eyes stared back at the burning blue of Moros's gaze. Nerves fluttered in his stomach, unsure of the expression across the God's face.

And how in the Fates he was responsible for it.

Moros gestured for Jes to sit at one of the armchairs placed on the opposite side of his glass desk.

Slowly, Jes nodded, backing up until his knees hit the seat of the chair. His hands trembled on the arms while he lowered himself, watching as Moros began to pace before the lit hearth warming the room.

"What are we?" Moros finally asked, his hand landing on the mantle of the hearth.

"What?" Jes questioned, cocking his head.

Moros's head threw back with an unamused laugh while his hair rippled in locks with the movement. "You heard my question, Jesiel. What. Are. WE?"

Jes's hands balled together, and his wings grew tight as his back. Why the sudden questioning? Why the need to determine anything?

All he needed was the peace his heart felt in Moros's presence.

Wasn't that enough?

"Jesiel!" Moros cried out, turning to face him.

Jes's mouth opened in shock at the tears running down Moros's face. But even more so how they froze right before hitting the ground.

Echoing across the study with devastating damage.

"I—" Jes shook his head. "Why does it matter?"

"Why?" Moros's voice grew distant. "Why does it matter?"

He turned back, leaning against the wall beside the hearth. "Am I your secret, Beskermer? Am I the newest conquest for you to keep hidden while you ride and fuck me for days on end like all the others? Only to never ask for me again?"

Jes stood, the chair clattered behind him. His wings snapped back with the rage rushing through his blood. "How dare you?" he seethed. "How dare you say something so carelessly?"

Moros crossed the room, laying his hands across the table. His determined gaze burned through Jes. Staring into the parts of his soul he'd kept locked up for so long.

The secrets he'd only revealed to the rage-filled man before him.

"What. Are. We?" Moros repeated.

Jes's mouth opened to respond but the words wouldn't form. His heart quickened the longer Moros held his gaze.

"I'm not going to live in secret, Jesiel!" Moros yelled, hands slamming against the glass table.

Jes stared at him, heart pounding, fear coursing through his blood. He knew he had to say everything that weighed on his heart. Every fear, every moment, every single thought Moros brought to his mind.

But he was terrified.

Moros scoffed at Jes's silence, flipping his hair behind his back. "For a fearless Beskermer, you are an absolute coward."

Jes fly across the table before he'd registered his body moving. The glass shattered with the force of the ends of his wings hitting it as he slammed Moros against the wall behind him.

His chest pressed against the cold body beneath him and Moros's gaze stared back in shock. His hands trembled beside Jes's thighs.

Tucking his silky black hair behind his ear, Jes stared into his lover's eyes. "I would do everything in my power to protect you, my *icy* man. You are no secret, but you are who I hold the most dear to my heart. Do not take my hesitancy to claim you publicly as me wanting to live in secret. I would wither into the deepest depths of Shadus if I ever lost you."

Moros's chest heaved against his own. Their hearts beat in harmony with one another's. The roar of the fire was now the only sound in the room.

Jes's hand rested above Moros's head while they kept their eyes locked on one another. And it was as though time had ceased to exist. Like at the valley. And that fateful night in the thick comforters of Moros's bed.

Just the two of them.

All that existed in that moment. Perhaps even in their world.

Jes's body trembled when Moros's hand suddenly rose, resting against his chest. His head dipped down, expecting the cold brush of lips against his own. Then he blinked in surprise when Moros was pushing him away.

Jes stepped back, wings straightening out behind him. The crush of glass beneath his boots filling the air.

"Moros..." Jes whispered.

Moros held up his hand, his eyes full of sorrow. "You didn't answer my question."

Jes's eyes widened, and his hands landed at his thighs in defeat.

"Was that not an answer?"

Moros shook his head. "No, Jesiel, that wasn't." his eyes went to the glass littering the room with its sparkle.

"Was it possibly the most attractive proclamation I've ever heard?" Moros's lip lifted briefly with a smile that tugged at Jes's heart. "Yes, Jesiel, you proclaimed *beautifully*. You just didn't answer my question."

Jes stepped back again. "What do you expect from me, Moros?"

Moros scoffed. "What do I expect? I expect to be loved loudly and openly, Jes."

"And what if I can't do that?" Jes whispered.

The silence that followed his question was deafening. Surrounding the two of them with palpable pain and despair. Jes kept his eyes downward while the air grew thick around them. He couldn't find the courage to look into the eyes of the person whose heart he'd likely just broken.

Moros cleared his throat. "Fine, then I must admit something to you."

Jes's head moved upward, barely meeting Moros's gaze. The rage staring back at him was enough for his Beskermer senses to switch on, the hairs on his body rising in response.

"What?" he demanded.

"You've failed to fulfill my needs of you. I was using *you, Jesiel.* Trying to get to Roan through you."

Jes balked, shaking his head with confusion.

"You what?"

Moros grinned that unnerving, unfeeling grin Jes had seen across both his and Marek's face far too many times. "I thought getting into the good graces of my cousin's closest friend would serve a purpose." Moros's tossed his hair back over his shoulder while his hand conjured a seat of thick snow.

Slowly, the God seated himself. Crossing his legs casually. "You have proved to be more of a distraction than a benefit. I have no more use of you."

Jes stared back in shock. "I can't believe you," he muttered.

Moros shrugged. "Everything I do has a purpose, Jes. I thought you'd have learned that by now."

Jes let out a scream and the wind responded, lifting the glass on the floor around them. "You're a pathetic, sad, little man, Moros." His wings beat behind him. "You *push*, you *pry*, and when you don't get your way you apparently throw a fit like a child."

Jes's hand moved, and Moros flinched in response. Pain gripped the Beskermer's heart at the response.

This God truly believed he would have harmed him.

Instead, Jes threw the glass behind him and out toward the windows overlooking Moros's city.

"All of this was a joke to you?" Jes questioned. "The secrets shared? The bed warmed with our bodies? Just to fulfill, what? Some game between you and that fucked up brother of Roan's?"

Moros stared back, unanswering. His hand tapping against the snow seat he sat upon.

Jes scoffed. "Fine then, Moros. You win your little game. You've bested the Beskermer. I hope whatever prize you were after is worth it."

"I told you I intended to get to Roan through you. I assure you that I receive no prize for your failure to fulfill your purpose," Moros replied coldly.

Jes stalked away, his heart cracking as he went. Throwing up his hands he yelled out over his shoulder, "To think, Moros. I was sure I was falling in love with you."

Moros stared after while Jes stormed out of the room. His tears froze down his face as they fell.

Balling his hands on the seat he'd made himself, he threw back his head, letting out a scream.

The palace shook with the sound, while thick clouds rolled over his city and Region. His season's response to the pain cracking across his heart. The rage at his own stupidity for believing that cold man could have loved him.

His screams echoed around him while he slammed his head back against his seat. The freezing tears sticking to his face as his storm raged around him.

He was sure he would freeze in his spot. Sure, his household would find him in the morning a frigid corpse of pain and anguish.

Of worthlessness.

His vision blurred the louder he screamed, and he was sure his body would give out when two strong, but petite hands, gripped his face.

"Moros," Riki whispered. "Moros."

"I've lost him," Moros muttered, burying his face against Riki's shoulder.

"Who, Moros?" She asked, holding him close.

"I've lost him," he repeated, closing his eyes with the image of Jes's heartbreak burned into his memory.

CHAPTER 14

Jes sat at the kitchen table, picking at his food, lost in his thoughts. A voice cleared across the room, and he glanced up to find Etta, Roan's housekeeper, standing at the door, eyeing him.

"Yes, Etta?" he questioned.

The small Godling woman stepped through the threshold, holding her stern gaze. Her feet quietly padded across the floor until she was beside him at the table. Her calloused hands wrapped around his.

Jes's chest tightened at the comfort of her touch while he offered her a smile.

"Something has changed in you," Etta observed, her brow raising.

"I—" Jes's words caught in his throat while he pulled his gaze away. He glanced around the quiet kitchen, wishing someone could save him from the woman's prying.

"Jes," Etta said softly, patting the top of his hand. "What stops you?"

Jes groaned, pulling away as he stood. "I have no idea what you're referring to, Etta," he replied.

He turned his gaze from hers, he wanted to get away. Remove himself from her knowing questions. He wanted to fly off to the camp and train until his body was ragged and bleeding.

He needed the rush of his pounding blood to drown out the thoughts threatening to pull him under.

Etta's hands wrapped arounds his and he shifted his eyes to stare into hers. He blinked, always surprised by the sparkles of white in her dark eyes. How it wasn't always there but when it did appear, it was magical.

Ironic considering he lived life surrounded by magic.

"My Jes," she whispered. "What stops you from being happy?"

His mouth opened to reply but he shook his head instead, unable to form the words.

"So much shame was trained into you," Etta muttered, patting the top of his hand. "You should ask those responsible why they did it."

Jes stepped back, eyes widening. "Etta," he warned. "Don't."

Etta gave him a stern scowl. "Why won't you just face what's inside of you, Jesiel? Why do you fight it?"

"Etta," he repeated. "I—" His shoulders sagged, "I can't."

"You believe you can't," she replied, approaching him once more. "But you have more strength inside then you give yourself credit for. Why not try?"

Jes glanced back at the kitchen entrance, wishing he had enough courage to leave this conversation. "I can't ask why they did this," he admitted. "The one who made me hate myself is no longer with us. Not unless I feel inclined to request an audience with the Fates." He shivered. "And I really do not feel inclined do that."

Etta grinned. "I don't think he's even with the Fates, dear."

Jes's mouth hung open as the housekeeper continued. "Go talk to her, Jes. She longs for you. Can't you feel it in the air? Doesn't her lament beckon you every time you take flight?"

Jes's lip trembled. He hated how accurate Etta was in her observation. Because she wasn't wrong. He did hear that voice in the wind. He felt the tug to return to his home in the trees. To the mother he'd long cut himself off from.

"How am I supposed to return? After so long?" Jes asked.

"No mother turns away their child," Etta replied. "At least no *good* mother."

She offered him a wink before walking out of the Kitchen.

Jes stared after her, his eyes traveling to the curved window overlooking the back lawn. He scanned the grass now covered in thick snow.

His heart tugged.

It was fully Moros's season now. The chill reaching into Jes's soul like it always had. Freezing his bones and blood in the most addicting way.

Only he couldn't run to it anymore. Not after that argument.

When he'd ended it. When he'd likely broken Moros in half with his harsh words.

Jes scoffed.

Contemplating who really hurt who. Remembering he'd just been a pawn in Moros's constant game of life. Likely deciding the conquest of a night with Roan's Beskermer to warm his bed to be the best prize of all.

After a few moments considering his choices, Jes crossed the kitchen. He'd been a coward for far too long. Allowing himself to stay secluded in this Region, following his Governing God around like a loyal servant.

Shutting himself away from the people who'd hurt him most, when he should have been standing up to them.

He slammed the side door open and the cold wrapped around his wings. His hands shook in response while the wind swirled around him, dancing between the sensitive feathers on his back. Tugging at those muscles to raise upward and launch him into the sky.

Glancing back at the Manor, he nodded once. A quiet acknowledgement of the duties he was bound to before flinging his body upward—toward Spreng.

Jes's body slammed into the warm earth, the dirt and rocks kicking up around his feet with his arrival. Shocked gasps and scattering echoed around him. Slowly, he pulled his eyes from the ground, focusing on tall wooden gates before him—the entrance to the Beskermer city.

Whispers filled the air while he stalked through the gates, not needing to worry about the wards to attack intruders. Not when his bloodline had created those wards.

"It's Jesiel," voices echoed.

"Alert her," others responded.

Jes let them mutter and point. He'd made a grand entrance on purpose. He wanted them all to know the prodigal son had returned.

He marched through the dirt streets of Tres, his wings held confidently behind him. He scoffed as he passed each canopied shop, his eyes glancing upward at the unmoving bodies on the bridges connecting each tree-top home together. The Beskermers own roadway.

Nothing had changed. The city was still as archaic as it always had been. In a world determined to evolve and change, the Beskermers kept themselves tucked away.

Teaching shame disguised as strength and duty.

Jes approached the main staircase of the city, the deep oak steps leading up to the branch bridges connecting the city together. His hands shook at his side while he focused through the thick canopy of leaves.

At the back of the village was the largest, oldest, and strongest towering Oak. With the circled halls he'd grown up running around and hanging branches he'd first been taught to launch himself from. His first place of both safety and torment.

His foot hit the bridge, and the wood groaned.

He glanced down, wondering if it were an indication that he had truly outgrown this city and its people. If the years of isolation and solitude had created an irreparable rift between who he was now and who he'd once been.

Shaking off the thought, he made his way through the winding branched streets, avoiding every gawking pair of eyes tracking him.

When he finally approached the Oak, his hands shook as he laid his palm against the rounded door carved into the stump.

Why halt, child? a familiar and brisk voice whispered through the wind.

Jes refused to answer as he shoved the door open, holding his head high as he stepped through the threshold of his childhood home. His feet carried him toward the double doors in the center of the house, throwing them open with force. Revealing the room where a stoic woman sat in a branch made throne, one hand resting on the arm, the other tapping her knee.

His mother—the queen of the Beskermers.

Jes studied her, his heart racing.

It had been a decade. Ten full years since he'd laid eyes on his mother, and he was shocked to realize he'd started to forget her features.

But she was before him now. The same stern golden gaze bearing into him, heavy with motherly expectations. Her dark skin shined under the canopied skylight above her. Nearly blending in with the branches that made up her throne. And her hair, longer than Jes had remembered, was braided back tightly.

Her large earrings rattled as her head shook and the bangles on her wrists clattered when her hands clapped together.

"You made quite the entrance, Jesiel." she said coldly, her white wings fanned out behind her as she stood.

Jes was rigid in his spot. His back aching as his wings fought the urge to lower in respect for his queen.

"I thought it would grab your attention, *Emani.*"

She jolted at the use of her first name before glancing out the towering windows beside him. Jes followed her gaze, watching as dozens of Beskermers scattered, their wings almost colliding with one another's.

"The city has been waiting for your return."

Jes held his composure as she stood. "I don't know why anyone is shocked to see me return."

His mother's anguish laid over the room while the wind shook the canopy above. "Honestly, Jesiel, I know you're smarter than that. When the child of the Queen and King of the Beskermers doesn't even show up to bid farewell to his own father, it would come as a shock to *anyone* for you to step foot in this city again."

Jes tucked his chin down as she approached. He felt how rough her hands were from years of training when they grasped his. But he couldn't... He wouldn't meet her gaze.

"What do you need?" she questioned. The tone of authority now shifting to one of a mother.

"I—" Jes pulled his hands away, stepping away. "I'm not sure why I'm here."

He walked toward the windows, staring down at the bodies moving about their days. His eyes traveled the length of the city until he found the encampment on the other side. The one he'd passed at the entrance, barely able to acknowledge its presence.

"I spent so many years down there," he whispered. "Being broken into obedience. To never question. To fight who I am in every sense."

"Jesiel," his mother's wind brushed against his wings, but he held up his hand.

"What was the cost, *mother?*" He turned, the word burning on his tongue. "Did you ever see it? Or did you choose ignorance at your own hands?"

"How dare you," she replied, her jeweled hands covering her lips. "You go silent for *years* and then saunter into *my* home and question my choices?"

Jes slammed his hands against the thick windowpanes. "I hate myself because of you! Because of him!" He met her gaze, finding tears lining her eyes. "You know why I didn't bid farewell. You know why I stayed away."

"If we were so awful," his mother replied, "why are you here? To throw our failures in my face? To bring me pain?"

Scoffing, Jes shook his head. "It's always been about you. Your image. How I'm perceived. How I fit into the image of the unyielding Queen and her people."

He left the windows, crossing to the small chairs on the opposite side of the room. He lowered himself, running his fingers over the table beside him and the worn wood. Remembering years in that seat, silently observing his parents.

His mother turned, her hand landing on her waist. Her shoulders slumped as the swishing of her long green gown echoed around them.

"Can we not argue? Can I relish in my child being home?"

Jes stared at the open doors, catching the brief flash of gold and white wings disappearing around the corner.

"How is she?"

His mother stilled. Her fingers twisted the bangles on her wrist. "She is fine."

Jes nodded as he made eye contact with his sister's bright eyes peeking from behind the door. Guilt rose in his throat, but he shoved it away.

He'd cut contact, believing his sister was better off without him in her life. Not when she was being trained up to lead the Beskermers one day. To be a hand of strength, loyalty, and protection.

Hi, Nat, he threw out to the wind, ignoring his mother's slight shift of her feet.

Nataki, to you, his sister replied sternly, but he grinned at the wink she threw his way.

"Jesiel," his mother interjected, snapping her fingers.

His sister yelped when the Queen's wind closed the doors. Sealing herself and her son in the room alone. Away from prying ears.

"Why have you returned?" she asked him again.

Jes met her eyes. "I needed my mother. If only for a moment. I needed to understand why you allowed me to believe the most important part of myself is the most shameful."

She stared at him blankly, her mouth slightly agape. "Jes—" Her words choked as she shook her head. "Sefu—"

Jes's hands balled together hearing his father's name for the first time in ten years.

His mother let out a shaky breath as she lowered to his level, her hand brushing his face. "I may be the queen. I may rule our people, but Sefu... He was my partner. He had ideals..." she sighed. "He had ideals that I have realized in recent years were harmful. He was rarely here with the duties he had to uphold, and I shouldn't have allowed his sternness to be beaten into you."

Jes pulled his face away. "I think I love someone, mother."

She let out a quiet noise, covering her lips. "Who is she?"

Jes turned to meet her eyes again. "*He* is the only person in my life who has never judged me for who I am."

The queen fell back, shaking her head while her tears fell. "Jesiel."

Jes stood, holding his hands up to stop her. "Your shock is enough confirmation." He moved to leave when her hands wrapped around his palm.

"No, please," she begged, pulling him back. "Please give me this chance."

"Do you really want to know who he is?" Jes replied, his heart racing at the admission he was about to make.

Her head lowered into a bow. "I would be honored to know."

"Moros," he answered quietly.

Her eyes went wide. "A Governing God, Jesiel!" she shouted, shaking her head. "Did losing your father teach you *nothing?*"

"My father taught me to hate myself!" Jes yelled back. "What does losing have to do with anything?"

His mother stepped forward, standing on the tips of her toes to grasp his face. "You put not only yours but his life in danger by being together, Jesiel." She sniffled. "Think about who you are bonded to. His Fate. His future. Where does Moros fit into all of that?"

Jes blinked. "Roan is the next God of Death."

His mother smiled. "While we Beskermers don't usually attend the challenges except those of us who are bonded, we have heard the whisperings."

Stepping back, Jes shook his head. "Stop," he commanded. His eyes glanced around the room, searching for the eyes and ears that were determined to bring Roan down. "No more."

The Queen of the Beskermers crossed the room, settling herself on her throne. "Roan's secret is safe here. We do not bow to the false King," she stated proudly. "That King is the reason I am living a life without my partner. I would cut down any coward who would run to him with information."

Jes stared in shock, blinking repeatedly while he tried to process her words.

"That being said," she leaned back on her throne, "what I say is true. You and I both know it. If Roan truly allows himself to take over our world, that puts a target on his back. Which in turns means there's a target on yours. The first place your enemies will look to are those you love most. A flighty Governing God who is rarely within the safety of his own Region would be the perfect target."

"Hold your tongue," Jes shot back, his rage burning to the surface.

"But," his mother's eyes shone, "from what I've heard, you and this Governing God are no longer on good terms."

Jes startled. "What?"

His mother shrugged. "Jesiel, I have eyes and ears all over this region. I have Beskermers at the side of every Governing God and Gods of power." She tapped her fingers against her throne. "When I heard of the storm that overtook Veturs last month, I was intrigued. Only, I didn't realize it was you who had broken that fragile, cold heart."

Jes's hand landed at his side, grasping for the sword he usually carried. But there was no weapon on his belt. A foolish mistake he'd never make again.

"Coming here was pointless," he replied coldly. "I expect you to keep the Beskermer duty of not uttering what was spoken of behind these closed doors."

His mother's eyes shone while she nodded. "I'm not the one who shirks my people's traditions, Jesiel."

The words bit into him, reminding him of why he'd stayed away.

"Don't let Nat turn into you," he threw back. "I think she may actually do some good for your ignorant ways."

Turning on his heels, he was almost to the doors when his mother's voice echoed around him. Circling with the wind determined to pull him back to her.

If you love him, Jesiel, you'll do the right thing. You'll protect him with your life. No matter the cost.

His shoulders stiffened and he refused to turn back. Grasping the door handles, he flung them open, silently saying goodbye to this city.

Severing the last threads of connection he had with his people.

CHAPTER 15

Moros walked the streets of Kall, grinning at the shrieks of the children playing in his storm. The heavy snow landed around him, layering his city with its beauty.

Fates how he loved the cold.

His breath puffed out before him and he glanced toward the top of the mountain, where his ice palace sat above the city. Glistening in the white of the storm.

While his heart ached and he was sure he'd never recover from the loss of Jesiel, he was content in the beauty of his home. He decided that, perhaps, he could take his duties and responsibilities as Governing God of this Region seriously for once. Maybe working with Riki would help him learn more about the ins and outs of his people.

Instead of ruling as an image and person of authority.

His eyes traveled his city, and he froze when a brief flash of gold and white came into his peripheral. His head whipped up toward his palace again, his heart racing at the large figure in the sky, circling his home.

Jesiel.

His heart leapt while he watched the winged figure circle the palace. As though the Beskermer was searching for him. He twisted his body and laid his eyes on the Perambulate. He could use the portal to get to the palace faster than attempting to run up the icy hill. He raced to the glass doors, pausing as his hand wrapped around the icicle handle.

Did Jes deserve him rushing frantically to his side? Did the man who refused to acknowledge what they were to each other require his immediate attention?

Moros's eyes went back to the sky. Tracking the man flying above, deciding he wasn't finished with his stroll around town. And the man who'd been so determined to leave him with biting words could wait as long as he deemed appropriate.

Moros made it to the top of the mountain, his feet aching and heart racing. He'd taken his time getting back home. Stopping and greeting his citizens. Playing in the snow with the younglings. Even accepting the warm tea his healer had offered.

But all the while he'd been aware of the figure in the sky. His mind going to the images of that dark skin against his own. The short, cropped hair. The wings intimately wrapped around his body while they lost themselves in each other's touch.

The lips—full and tempting.

No, Moros hadn't been able to distract his thoughts away from the Beskermer Jesiel. The giant winged man that was determined to keep this—whatever it was—a secret.

And it drove the God absolutely mad.

He reached for his front door, jumping back when it slammed open and Riki stared at him with wide eyes.

"Jesiel has been circling this palace for *hours*," she exclaimed. "Where were you?"

Moros brushed past, hanging his thick jacket on the hook near the door. "Why didn't you come for me?"

Riki scoffed. "And leave that brooding giant to attack?"

Moros laughed, flinging his hair over his shoulder. "He wouldn't attack."

He continued to walk when Riki's hand grasped his forearm, pulling him back. "I know."

"Know what Riki?" Moros turned on his heel slowly, his voice dipping into authority.

Riki stared back, holding her small frame confidently. "I know he's who holds your heart."

Moros held up his hand. "Enough."

"No." Riki stepped forward, her eyes glancing down the hall toward the balcony. "He went to her."

Moros stepped back. "What?"

"The man who hasn't rested once in hours went to his mother, Moros. He—"

Moros cut her off, gripping her shoulders and shaking her. "He what? What Riki?"

"I don't know, I just know Nat said he spoke with their mother for at least an hour and when he left, she wept on her throne."

Moros released his Beskermer, and his feet propelled him through his palace. His hands slammed the balcony doors open, and he turned, heading for the ice stairway that led to the roof.

His hands grew slick with sweat, the liquid freezing on his palm as he raced upward.

When he reached the roof, he lifted his head. High in the sky, amongst his still raging snowstorm was Jesiel. A picture of beauty, grace, and duty. Circling the ice palace like a predator searching for his prey.

"Beskermer!" Moros shouted, booming his voice over the wind of the storm.

Jes's body dropped so quickly Moros could barely track him. Then he was before him, his broad chest heaving, his wings relaxed and brushing against the cold roof.

"God," Jes said briskly.

Moros shook while he stared into the burning golden eyes before him. He was angry. So angry he was sure he'd break apart.

But he was also relieved.

Because Jes had come back—for him.

"Kiss me you, brute," Moros finally said, repeating the words he'd said before.

Jes was on him in an instant, slamming their bodies against the edge of the roof. His fingers tangled in Moros's hair as their lips collided.

The heat of him against Moros's own cold skin was as addicting as before. Two opposites, complimenting each other. Both of them determined to warm their bodies while cooling themselves at the same time.

Moros wrapped his hands around Jes's neck, moving his lips in sync. He needed this. He needed to feel the desire for the man who had gripped his heart.

He needed the power rushing through him, knowing that man had returned to him.

They fell together, landing on the roof while Jes's wings wrapped around them as their bodies tumbled. Moros's hair fell around them, creating another blanket as Jes's hands explored, running down Moros's back, pulling at his top. His hot hand lay flat against Moros's stomach.

Moros's head fell back as Jes's lips found his neck, his fingers playing with the edges of his trousers.

Then his eyes snapped open. And the rage returned.

Moros wiggled away, straightening his clothes and hair before glaring at the disheveled looking Beskermer still laying on the ground.

"What?" Jes asked, head shaking. "What in the Fates in wrong with you?"

"Me?" Moros proclaimed? "What's wrong with me?"

As quickly as he'd run up there, he was suddenly rushing across the roof and back down the stairs. His mind was reeling. His body was aching for release. But his heart was tight, full of rage, and begging for a fight.

The fumbling sounds of Jes chasing after him ignited his blood as he rushed down his halls, passing a shocked Riki. He rushed around the corner, past his study, and heading straight for his bedroom.

He flew up the solitary staircase to the bedroom at the top of the spire. Jes's echoing footsteps getting closer were followed by Riki's yelling after both of them.

But he didn't stop.

Moros slammed his bedroom open, running to the opposite side, balling his fists as he watched the threshold.

Moments later Jes stepped through the door. His eyes wild with frustration.

"Moros," the Beskermer hissed.

"Jesiel," Moros replied.

The door slammed shut behind Jes and he was crossing the room in an instant. Moros watched as his large body moved toward him. His wings propelling him off the ground.

Jes shoved him against the wall, his arms resting right above his head.

"Why did you run from me?" Jes asked, his nose barely touching Moros's.

"You ran away first," Moros replied.

Jes was silent while they held their gazes. Then his hand dropped, and he stepped back. Moros leaned against the wall watching Jes sink onto his lush bed.

"I love you," Jes whispered.

Moros's response choked in his throat. A relieved, yet terrified haze fogged his mind. The three words that had hammered into his heart were being reciprocated.

So why didn't he feel anything other than sorrow?

"Why do you love me?" he finally forced himself to ask.

Jes's head turned, his eyes shimmering with emotions. "You see me, Moros. You knew a part of me since that day on the balcony. You—" Jes smiled. "You broke into my mind and heart so quickly I thought I was going crazy. Your touch was like the burn of a cold fire and my body held onto it for days."

Moros blinked, his mind going back to his teasing caress at the Palace of Nyte. How he hadn't been able to stop himself from trailing his fingers across Jes's beautiful muscles. Like some nymph had taken control of him.

Jes stood. "Every moment I haven't been with you has been torture. It's been—" His voice trailed off while his shoulders slumped. "I told my mother about you."

Moros stared back, shock rippling through his body.

"You went home?"

"I did," Jes replied quietly. "I won't return again, but I had to prove to her that I wasn't the Beskermer she was determined to mold me into."

Moros considered his words.

"I don't know why you told her about me when you refuse to acknowledge what we are."

Jes's head cocked. "I don't know why you're acting as though you've done nothing wrong."

Moros glared back. The Beskermer was besting him at his own game and as thrilling as it was, he hated it.

Shrugging, he winked as he tossed his hair back. "I had my own agenda, I'll admit that."

"Was it all pretend?" Jes asked.

Moros's smug grin fell from his lips. "No, Jes." he let out a breath. "I've been as smitten and enamored with you as you've been with me."

He pushed off the wall, joining the large man on his bed. Turning his gaze, Moros gripped Jes's hand. "We seem to be in a predicament."

Jes's head cocked. "How so?"

Moros laughed. "Am I wrong to assume you telling your mother was behind a closed door known to seal in Beskermer *secrets?*"

Jes gawked. "How did you—"

"Riki," Moros cut him off. "We talk, you know. Actually took a page out of yours and Roan's friendship with my Beskermer. I was inspired by the two of you years ago."

Jes was silent, his hand tightening around Moros's grip.

"I'm trying," he whispered.

Moros stared at him. His brief amusement by Jes's discomfort replaced with empathy.

It had been so long, close to centuries, since he'd felt any shame in who he was. So long ago that somedays he barely remembered the young boy terrified to tell his mother about his first relationship.

But as he gazed upon the usually confident man shrinking before him, he remembered all too clearly how terrifying it was.

"Tell me about yourself, Jes."

Jes turned to him, his throat visibly bobbing with emotion.

"I'm scared."

Moros stood, placing himself before Jes then sinking to his knees.

"I know your father was a hard, judgmental man," Moros whispered. His hands laid on Jes's lap and Jes let out a startled gasp. "I know you're bound by your Beskermer bond."

Moros trailed his hands up Jes's rigid body, his fingers brushing across his jawline. Jes leaned into his touch and Moros breathed in his scent.

He smelled like snow, fire, and home.

"I can see you believe something isn't right with you because you can enjoy my body and a woman's body."

Jes's eyes went wide. "Moros—"

Moros cut him off, placing a gentle kiss on his lips. "I don't care, Jesiel. I don't care."

Jes's hands gripped his face while his lips moved in response.

"I don't care," Moros whispered. Repeating the words while they kissed each other softly.

"I'm sorry," Jes whispered back, pulling at Moros's shirt. "I'm so sorry."

Moros fell on top of his winged man, allowing those massive wings to envelop them both. To guard them against the weights of their world, roles, and duties. Welcoming the soft feathers to blanket them both in each other.

His hands moved against Jes's body, pulling at the edge of his shirt. And Jes moved willingly, sitting up while Moros unbuttoned the sides, allowing the shirt designed for wings to fall off the magnificent body.

Staring at Jes's bare chest, Moros's cheeks grew hot at the tension aching low. Jes's eyes traveled down his body, landing on the desire straining against his trousers.

"Take those off," Jes demanded, pointing with a smirk on his lips.

"Is that an order?" Moros replied.

He yelped when Jes grabbed him, pinning him to the bed. His hands quickly pulling the buttons off the trousers. The sound of the metal echoing as the button bounced across the bedroom floor.

Moros stared into his golden eyes, his body shaking as Jes slowly pulled the fabric from his body. The cold of his room forced Moros to take a sharp inhale when his skin was exposed. His hands gripped his comforter, watching as Jes stared down at him.

"You are magnificent," Jes mumbled, dropping to his knees.

"Jes," Moros protested, his body aching for more. "Jes," he repeated as Jes's lips trailed up his legs.

"I am yours," Jes whispered, his hands slipping past the hem of Moros's shirt and landing on his lower stomach.

Moros groaned, throwing his head back as the heat of Jes's lips wrapped around him.

"Fates," he exclaimed, his hips bucking at the swish of Jes's tongue against the tip of him.

All control he had, all restraint to fight off his need to be touched by the Beskermer that had infiltrated his mind, disappeared while Jes's mouth moved expertly. Washing away the pain still swelling in his heart and the uncertainty of the future slipping into the recesses of his mind.

His senses fell with him as his body accepted the ecstasy of Jes's touch and the words he continued to repeat.

"I am yours."

CHAPTER 16

ONE YEAR AFTER CHALLENGE

Jes stroked long, dark hair while the man it belonged to slept against his chest. His eyes scanned the room surrounding him. The thick comforter warming them both, and the always burning fire blazing in the hearth.

It had been months of this. Sleeping every few nights in the safety of Moros's home. Welcoming the God's touch with no regard for being caught. No care that he left his Governing God unprotected each night.

It had been hard at first, his duty and Beskermer nature commanding him to return to the Manor. But after a few weeks, it had become second nature.

Retiring to bed, waiting until the Manor was totally silent, and then slipping out the side door taking the Perambulate to the portal in Moros's study.

Moros shifted in his sleep and Jes's heart clenched.

He was so inexplicably in love with the man sleeping peacefully against him. But he was still so scared. Terrified of what would happen if he claimed this man as his own.

What could happen if those who were determined to bring down his bonded found out about him.

"What's wrong?" Moros's sleepy voice asked as he sat up.

Jes smiled at him, tucking a piece of his disheveled hair behind his ears. "Nothing," he lied.

Moros scowled. "Your heart sounded as though it were going to beat out of your chest. What's wrong?"

Jes sighed. "Does Marek know about us?"

Moros froze.

"Moros?" Jes questioned.

Moros sat straighter, twisting his hair into a bun atop his head. "No," he said curtly. "No, he does not."

"I thought he was your closest friend," Jes replied, sitting up.

Moros scowled at him. "Your closest friend doesn't know either, Jesiel. Let's not forget that."

Jes held up his hands. "I'm not trying to argue," he sighed. "I was only curious. What happens if he finds out? Will you ever tell him?"

Moros was silent as he slipped off the bed, wrapping a black silk robe around his body. "Marek doesn't know everything about me."

"That doesn't sound like friendship."

"Why all the questioning this morning?" Moros groaned. His eyes went to a small clock on his bedside. "Don't you have to get back?"

The last question left his lips with a small squeak. Jes dropped his head with guilt, glancing at the time.

"Fates," he muttered. "We slept in."

"Better go then," Moros snapped, turning on his heel toward the bathroom. "Wouldn't want to keep *Roany* waiting."

"Moros," Jes called out, but Moros only held up his hand to stop him.

"I'm going to be busy with Wintur ending. I have to go discuss the shift with Dagny. My yearly trip to Spreng."

Jes blinked. "What?"

"I won't be here, Jesiel," Moros replied over his shoulder. "Stay in Nacht until I send after you."

Jes stared as Moros shut the bathroom door behind him. Creating an obvious barrier between the two of them, efficiently ending the conversation.

Jes stood from the bed and grabbed his clothes and dressed quickly. What Moros didn't know is that Roan wouldn't be waiting for him. Because for the last year, Roan was used to his Beskermer being gone each morning and for most of the day.

Only appearing when Roan called for him through the wind or in the weekly meetings with the officials.

No, Jes only left Moros so early each morning out of fear. Because he didn't know how to explain to Roan where he was coming from.

Like a coward.

Jes trudged through the Palace of Wintur, keeping close to the shadows, hoping to avoid any of Moros's staff. He rounded the corner, almost making it to the study when soft footsteps approached.

"Slinking away again?" his cousin's judging voice asked.

Jes rolled his eyes, staring down at the scowl on Riki's face.

"He sent me away. Claimed he'll be in Spreng for the foreseeable future."

Riki laughed. "That's actually true. I was coming to tell him Dagny is expecting him in the next hour."

Jes smiled. "Well, I hope you both have a good trip." He turned back toward the study, hoping the get through the portal as quickly as he could but Riki's voice cleared.

"Yes, Riki?" Jes asked, twisting his body to face her again.

"It's been months, Jes," Riki replied. "Why are you two still living in secret?"

"I guess we both have people we fear to find out about what we are."

"What are you?" she asked, her brow raising.

Jes's heart twinged at the question. His eyes traveled beyond his cousin's head, tracking where the hallway led to a spiraled staircase. Where a likely annoyed with him God was readying for the day.

"I'm in love with him," Jes admitted, shifting his gaze back to his cousin.

Riki stared back at him, shock evident on her face. "He didn't betray Roan."

Jes stepped back. "What?"

Riki sighed. "You heard what I said, Jesiel. Moros doesn't have a traitorous bone in his body. Everything that God does is for a reason."

Her eyes glanced backward nervously. "You know there's only so much I can say before the Beskermer bond prevents me from revealing my God's secrets." Her voice shook. "If you are any ounce of the Beskermer I think you are, ask your God the truth. I beg of you."

Jes stared in shock as Riki darted down the hall. Her small wings bouncing with her retreat.

He turned on his heel, rushing the opposite way. A newfound confidence rushed through him as he prepared to question his Governing God.

▢▢▢

Jes made it back to the Manor, finding Roan's study empty. His eyes laid on the newly formed door behind Roan's desk. The door that hadn't been there ten years prior when they'd first settled into the Manor.

Fates, the door hadn't even been there a year ago.

Jes made his way across the room, hesitantly entering Roan's recently constructed library. What had once been hidden servants and household quarters, now turned into Roan's own personal escape.

Jes scanned the room, finding Roan thumbing through a small collection of books. Jes stopped, watching his friend flip through the pages of hand-written notes from the Queen they'd all lost a decade before.

"Roan?" Jes said quietly.

Roan startled in his chair, his hand running through his hair before he shut the book he held.

"Everything alright?"

Jes stared at his friend, guilt eating at him with the knowledge that Roan was surprised to see him at this time of day because Jes had spent the last year angry and sneaking around.

Creating distance between himself and his brother.

"Can we talk?" Jes asked, pointing to the couches in the windows.

Roan's head scanned the still empty shelves of his library, and he nodded, standing slowly.

Together they sat down, both fidgeting nervously.

"Are we actually going to talk or are you going to beat the shit out of me again?" Roan asked with a grin.

Jes laughed, slapping his knee. "Fuck you."

"Wouldn't you just *love* to," Roan winked.

"I'm sorry," Jes muttered in response.

Roan was silent beside him.

"I've been too harsh with you," Jes replied. "I've let my personal beliefs and feelings get in the way of our friendship. I let myself come between our bond."

He glanced over, finding Roan staring out the window.

"There are some days when I question why I didn't fight," Roan whispered. "Some days when I wonder if I should have done better. If I should have allowed myself to become the Governing God of Daee and prove my Father wrong."

Jes leaned back, allowing his friend to open up.

"But," Roan turned his gaze back to Jes. "Most days I stare out at this beautiful city. At the peace of it all. The sky that I so easily control and the stars I paint the world with, and I realize the Fates have a plan for everything.

"I didn't mean to throw the challenge as a way to punish us, Jes." Roan sighed. "Yes, I wanted to make that monster realize I was powerful enough to best a Fate created challenge, but that also means the Fates allowed me to do so."

Jes contemplated the words, realizing he hadn't considered that stance in the time since the challenge had occurred. His mind went over all that had happened in the last year. The love he'd found and how that likely wouldn't have happened if Moros hadn't appeared on the balcony that night.

"I didn't realize," he whispered, voicing his inner thoughts.

Roan nodded. "I hadn't come to that conclusion until recently. Considering how much time I've spent alone in my thoughts."

"Way to make a good moment between us turn into a reminder that I've been an ass," Jes laughed.

"I've been an ass as well," Roan chuckled. "At least we're even."

Roan stuck out his hand for Jes to take. But Jes stared down at it, not sure if he could concede just yet.

"I have a question that's been eating at me lately."

Roan pulled his hand back, his brow raising. "Yes?"

"What happened between you, Marek, and Moros? I know it was before we met in Guerra. But what was it?"

Roan stood, his irritation evident with the lights dimming around them. "Look who's ruining a good moment," he sighed. "I don't want to talk about that."

"Roan," Jes pried. "I'm your Beskermer. I'm bound to keep your secrets. I'm bound to protect you. And most importantly, I've always been your friend first."

"Marek is a monster," Roan replied.

"I know this."

"No," Roan's hands trembled. "You don't."

"What happened?"

Roan stared out the windows behind Jes, his face shifting to a disgusted scowl. "I was sent to Guerra after Marek and Arno bonded. But not until there was a party held in his honor. My Father wanted to celebrate Marek bonding to the largest Beskermer known to recent history."

Jes rolled his eyes. Remembering his cousin proudly boasting the King's celebration for his accomplishment bonding to the next-in-line.

"That night…" Roan's voice trailed off. "That night I think is the night my brother started slipping into his depravities."

Jes's breath hitched in his throat while he listened, refusing to believe where Roan was going.

"I happened upon him and her. Her terrified tears are forever burned into my memories while he trapped her in his flames, burning her clothes from her body but never burning her skin."

"That fucker," Jes snarled.

Roan held up his hand. "I ran for Moros. My older cousin. The only one I knew who had the power to put out those flames."

"And?"

"And he came, he put out those flames, but then he forced me away. Demanding I *keep my fucking mouth shut*."

Jes blinked. "Then what?"

Roan scowled. "What do you mean?"

"That's it?"

"Jesiel Keita, I just told you Moros did nothing to help that young woman and you're asking if *that's it?*"

"I—" Jes stared off into the distance, trying to piece it all together. "You've always claimed that Moros is a traitor. That he betrayed your trust. How was this betraying your trust? What happened to the girl?"

"The girl was a mortal," Roan scoffed. "Marek has always been infatuated with mortals." He sat back down beside Jes. "I'm actually not sure what happened to her. I only know that both Moros and Marek claimed I was a liar when I told my parents what I'd seen. So yes Jesiel, Moros did betray me."

Jes sighed. "And you've never asked him what happened?"

"I tried countless times. But he began to treat me like the younger cousin who wasn't worth his time. He brushed me off, sticking close to Marek and following him around like some lackey obsessed with the *rightful heir*."

Jes laid his head against the back of the couch. His eyes staring at the ceiling above.

"That God is one that can't be trusted," Roan said beside him. "He always has an agenda. He will always do what he believes benefits him. I can recognize that he saved an innocent life, but I can't accept why he allowed Marek to get away with it."

"I can't either," Jes whispered.

Roan stood again, wiping his pant legs. "What do you say about a drink at the pub?"

Jes turned his gaze back to his friend, pain clenching in his chest.

"Are you alright?" Roan asked, his smile dropping.

"I thought we agreed you can't read my emotions," Jes replied, standing quickly.

Roan grinned. "You made it too easy. Are you alright?"

"I'm fine," Jes replied. "Drinks?" he asked pointing out to the study.

"Drinks my friend," Roan smiled, clasping his hand across Jes's back as they walked out the library.

Jes's mind reeled as they walked. The duty bond in him demanded he listen to his Governing God's warning. But the other bond, nestled deep inside of him, the one that led him to strong, cold arms, begged him to fight.

Even if it was the last thing he did.

CHAPTER 17

M oros walked through the Palace of Spreng, admiring the canopied
ceilings above. His eyes took in the space around him. The green-
ery, the flowers, the scents—almost intoxicating.

He was lost admiring the beauty when a quiet voice cleared behind him.
Turning he met the eyes of the Goddess of Spring.

"Dagny," he said, bowing his head in respect.

Dagny's long red hair rippled with her responding laugh. "Come now,
Moros. Even after decades of these yearly visits, I would have thought the
formality could cease by now."

Moros lifted his head. "You can only do so much when the formality is
trained into you at such a young age."

Dagny's smile dropped and she nodded. Approaching him, she looped
her arm around his. "We're one of the unlucky ones who were raised in this
life of aristocracy." She pulled them down her long green hallway as she
continued. "Me, raised as a child of generations of Gods and Goddesses of
Spring and you..." She met his gaze. "A child of two Governing Gods, one
a child of a King."

Moros removed his arm from hers as he held his back straight. "Duty
and family have a benefit."

"Does it?" Dagny asked.

The question stopped Moros in his tracks. He turned, placing a hand on
his hip. Crumpling his brow, he stared at the Goddess.

"You know, there are many in this world who would consider that
treason."

Dagny's green eyes lit with amusement. "Come now, Moros. It's just you
and I in this hallway. Two Governing Gods discussing the workings of our
Regions and the changing hands of our seasons."

"We had that discussion weeks ago," Moros replied.

Dagny grinned. "And yet you're still here, wandering the halls of my palace. Almost freezing my newly budding blossoms."

"If you'd like me to leave, then you can say so," Moros answered.

Dagny shook her head while a sly smile crept up her lips. "No, Moros you are always welcome to stay as long as you want." Her hand moved, reaching into an unseen pocket of her gown. When she pulled it out, Moros groaned, recognizing the scroll.

Dagny handed it to him. "Your duty—your mother has requested your audience."

Moros ripped the paper from the Goddess, letting out his complaints. "If only I were as lucky as you to have certain duties returned to the Fates."

"Moros," Dagny gasped, her fingers went to her lips. "Don't speak so callously of death. I know your Father was nothing to admire, but your mother? Our world would be lost without her."

Shame crept through Moros, and he hung his head. "I know." His fingers unrolled the scroll. "The trust is, I would be lost without her as well."

Dagny patted his hand. "I'll see you next year?"

"What?" Moros glanced up from his mother's note, registering what Dagny had said. He offered a smile then nodded his head. "Yes, my friend. I'll see you next year."

Dagny left him alone in the hall while he scanned his mother's request. It was simple, almost too simple. Just two words. No signature.

Come home.

Moros rolled up the scroll, realizing Dagny had been leading him toward the bedroom he'd been staying in. Laughing, Moros shook his head and pushed open the door.

He had to pack. He had to leave.

Because other duties required his attendance, and he would welcome extending his trip to avoid the brooding Beskermer waiting for his word to come back to him.

As he stepped through the portal in the Palace of Wisdom, Moros groaned when his heavy bags hit the ground.

"Why don't you ward them to follow?" his mother asked off to the side.

Moros jumped at her voice. "Fates, mother!" he exclaimed. "Why are you so intent on startling me every time I visit."

He turned his head to find an amused smile on his mother's lips. Unable to hold back his own grin, he shook his head.

"Despite the years of you teaching me wards, I do prefer some manual labor every now and then."

"That seems useless," the Goddess of Wisdom replied, snapping her fingers.

The swishing of robes entered the foyer, and Moros rolled his eyes at the scholar now answering his Mother's beckoning. She pointed to his bags, not uttering one sound and as always, the scholars understood. Like some unspoken language existed between her and her people.

Moros watched, leaning back against the wall. He never understood how she did it. Commanding with such power and grace while holding a fair and just hand.

It was admirable. While also maddening when he considered his Father's ruling of Veturs and how Moros was barely gaining trust from his own citizens.

His mother's voice pulled him from his thoughts. "Are you lost?"

"Don't do that," Moros replied, pushing away from the wall.

"Wisdom isn't always a welcome gift," Amada replied. "There are not always days when I want to be so equipped with observation that it forces me to say things I likely shouldn't."

Moros refused to reply. Instead, he crossed the foyer to the open sitting room doors on the other side. As he crossed the threshold, the old wooden floors creaking beneath his feet, he breathed in the familiar scent.

His mother's always burning hearth was lit with the walls lined with books. The smell welcoming, comforting. Stories that Moros spent his youth lost in. Friends he'd made in fables from long ago. Worlds he wished existed.

All still there, waiting for him.

Sinking into the dark brown couch, Moros lifted his feet onto the ottoman while his mother's quiet steps entered the room behind him.

He waited until she joined him on the couch, her hand resting against the cushion between them.

"How are things?" she asked, glancing at him.

Moros threw his head back with a laugh. "Mother, things are *well.*"

Amada studied him, her eyes moving from his head to his toes. "Why lie?"

"Mother," he groaned, straightening himself. "Did you call for me to interrogate me? If so, I'm going to take those packs back and just head home. My duties with Dagny and Spreng have been completed. I can let my season and Region rest for a while."

His mother shook her head. "No, Moros. I only wanted to know how *you* are."

Moros stood, heading toward the closest book-lined wall. His hands ran across the spines. The quiet whispers of the stories kicked up around him at his touch. Like the books themselves were in need of eyes to read their words.

"Why did you love him?" he asked quietly.

"Oh," his mother whispered. "Moros."

"Please, mother." Moros turned back to her glistening gaze. "You asked me months ago why I let a man cause me pain. But..." His heart tightened. "I watched you go through pain. Constant pain and you always went back to him. Always ran into those cold arms that caused so much destruction."

Amada leaned back against the couch and Moros startled at the way his usually stoic and graceful mother's shoulders sagged. Her hand went to her head while a tear left the corner of one eye.

"I met him when I was barely out of my adolescence. Running from the madness of my Father and the feud he fueled between my brothers. I ran right into those cold arms, desperate for them to bring me warmth."

Moros set the book down, his body buzzing while his mother talked. Never in his long life had she spoken so freely. And the air in the room appeared to still while the words left her mouth. A momentous occasion for such open conversation.

"He wasn't always cold," she continued, meeting Moros's shocked gaze. "When we first met, Moros... Oh Fates was he the sanctuary my soul needed."

"Fate bound?" Moros whispered. Refusing to acknowledge the sacred love granted by the Fates had been the love his mother had for his father.

She shook her head. "No, Moros. Not fate bound. Thank the Fates for that. But I thought it was. For many years it felt akin to that. Then..."

Moros returned to the couch, grasping her hands. She turned, giving him a little squeeze.

"Then the woman who followed him with little question. The woman who warmed his bed and looked away from his rampages of rage on his people was gifted a Region. Equal power to his—more power than his—and everything changed."

Moros dropped her hand. "He was a monster."

"He was a tormented soul given power far too young and not guided through it correctly. He was surrounded by men ruling this world for far too long. You have to remember, until my Godhood, the only other Goddess in almost a Millennia was Irie. But she stays hidden in her autumn oasis only meeting when required."

Moros grinned thinking about the quirky Goddess living amongst her yellow and orange trees.

He sat straighter, returning his thoughts to the conversation before him.

"How long do you think love should be painful for?"

"Why are you asking?" his mother replied with a smirk.

"Mother," Moros groaned.

"However long you wish to allow it, Moros." She laughed at the scowl on his face while her hand patted the top of his. "That's the honest answer, my darling. You have the control, even if your heart tells you otherwise."

Moros let out a breath. "I have to admit something."

"Yes?"

"I get upset with..." he glanced at her before clearing his throat, "*him*... because I understand his fears. I understand the idea of duty getting in the way of joy."

"What duty stops you?"

Moros shook his head, lifting his hand. "I can't."

"Alright," she replied, and Moros let out a breath, grateful for her ability to know when to stop her questioning.

"I understand why he's scared. I see the hate and shame he has in himself. And I can't fault him for it. Not with how he was raised. Not with what he's always known. I just wonder..."

"How long you can take it for?" she interjected.

Moros nodded, his heart twisting in agony inside of himself. He hated that he had caused so many fights with Jesiel when he had this secret inside of him all this time. That he had caused the giant of a man so much pain because Moros hated how much he related to those fears.

Causing useless rifts between them. Focused on gaining the upper-hand and completing his agenda. When in reality, his heart had been cracking open to that winged brute, wanting him always despite everything.

"Moros," his mother patted his hand again. "What do you want?"

"Him," Moros whispered, tears falling from his eyes. "I want *him*. In whatever facet that comes to. In whatever way I can. For as long as I live."

The Goddess stood suddenly, and Moros watched her pace the room. Not in a frantic way, but as though she were pondering the right words to say.

"Love can be painful. I've seen it personally and I've watched those I love experience some of the most painfully, heartbreaking love imaginable."

Moros cocked his head. "Who?"

Amada offered him a sad smile while her eyes drifted to the portraits on the mantle. Moros followed her gaze, his eyes landing on the round portrait at the end. Where a smiling painting of his late aunt smiled back at him.

"Leora?" he asked, shocked.

"My brother," Amada tsked her tongue with disapproval. "Fates, I wonder if he's not the worst monster amongst us all. That love between him and his fate bound, oh my son, was it painful. I watched that woman fight that pain every day of her life for herself and her children."

"This isn't inspirational," Moros interrupted.

Amada held up her hand. "I wasn't done. I would ask her. Every time I saw her if she could leave. If she could stop that pain, and she always refused. Because she loved him. Even through the madness and rage, she had found something inside of that man that no one else could see."

She returned to the couch, crouching before her son. "Roan, Marek, and Lahana had a mother who was stronger than anyone knows, and she made choices." Moros's mother grasped his hands. "What choices are you going to make, Moros? Have you found someone whose heart only you can see?"

Moros stared down at her hands, refusing to let them go. Tears built in his eyes when he finally lifted his gaze to hers.

"Mother," he sobbed. "I think I've found the only man who has ever seen *my heart*."

"Then, my son," his mother whispered, "what are you going to do about that?"

CHAPTER 18

J es flew through the cold air of Veturs, surprised he'd been able to force himself to complete the hours-long journey without turning back like a coward. His eyes tracked the white terrain, scanning over the smoke billowing from the chimneys of the small houses below him.

His wings fanned out as he circled high above the city of Kall, contemplating his next move. He'd spent the last several weeks waiting for Moros to send word. And as the days had dragged on, he'd begun to wonder if maybe the man would never call for him again.

Maybe they both were supposed to acknowledge their inability to be together publicly. Both of them bound to silent duties and loyalty outside of their control.

But then the letter had appeared. Wafting through Jes's open bedroom window on the last frigid wind of Wintur.

The valley.

Just two simple words, but Jes had known what they meant. Only, his fear had prevented him from taking the city portal. No, instead, he took flight, allowing the hours for him to wonder what lay ahead for him and his future.

Jes turned his focus away from the city below, shifting it to the mountain range behind the palace. Where he knew an icy man waited for him. Likely wrapped in the faux furs in a cabin hidden from the world.

Beating his wings, Jes propelled through the air. Nerves racking through him.

He landed on the alcove, eyeing the dark cave it led into.

He hated the dark. Fates how he hated the dark, but to his surprise the further he walked, the brighter it became.

Jes's hands trembled while he brushed against the twinkling warded lights guiding his way and the little notes carved into the ice.

Hurry up.

You're so slow.

I'm naked.

No, really.

Please hurry you brute.

By the time he found himself before the entrance to the valley, he was nearly in tears from laughter. Moros's humor was unique and entirely his own.

Another reason why Jes had fallen hopelessly in love with the man.

Jes shook nervously, staring at the falling water that Jes had once seen Moros change from bright blue ice,. His head told him he was only visiting Moros in the most peaceful place they had access to. But his heart...

His heart wondered if this was possibly goodbye. A melancholy farewell.

"You're taking too long," a teasing voice came from behind the water.

Jes startled, stepping back as Moros stepped forward with the water parting around him in beautiful streams.

"I waited naked in that cabin for *days*," Moros winked.

Jes chuckled. "Surprising, considering I received your note only this morning."

Moros shrugged. "I thought the allure of my body would have alerted those Beskermer senses."

"Get over here," Jes replied.

Moros crossed the small space, his cold approaching like an incoming storm. Jes grabbed the back of his neck, pulling the God toward him.

"We have much to discuss," he whispered.

Moros stared back at him. The blue of his eyes swirling with heat and desire. A kind of burn Jes could barely resist.

"Yes we do," he replied, placing his hand on Jes's chest.

Jes pulled away, trying to clear his head. With a tilt of his chin, he grunted. "The cabin?"

Moros's head shook, his hair moving in waves. He cleared his throat. "Yes, the cabin. I have food for us."

Jes stepped forward, ready to lead the way when Moros's hand wrapped around his.

"Can we just walk, slowly, with no requirements? I've spent weeks on a schedule."

Staring down at the hand in his, Jes nodded. He offered a soft smile before squeezing tightly. "Yes, let's just walk. No rush."

They walked silently while Jes marveled at the valley, amazed he had already forgotten how majestic it was. Even more so how not one other soul besides the two of them appeared to know of its existence.

Moros's free hand moved while they walked and Jes admired the light snow falling from his palm. How each snowflake was unique. Just like the God whose other hand gripped his so tightly.

When they finally made it down the curving path and across the terrifying frozen lake, Jes opened the cabin door. The smell of warm bread and hearty meat hit his nose, and he let out a breath of relief.

So far, nothing had indicated that this special thing between the two of them was ending.

He settled into the faux furs on the floor, watching as Moros gathered the meal he'd brought.

"I have a question," Moros said as he lowered to the ground, holding the tray in his hands carefully.

Jes reached up, helping him lower the tray of bread, stew, and what appeared to be mulled wine to the ground.

"I have an answer."

Moros smirked. "The Beskermer has jokes."

Jes winked. "I try."

Moros nestled up next to him, offering Jes the warm mug. Jes took it, grateful for the heat to warm his frozen fingers.

"Beskermers don't approve of the use of furs," Moros said, sipping on his drink.

Jes's glanced at him. "That's not a question."

"I wasn't done."

"Alright," Jes laughed. "Carry on."

Moros sipped from his cup again and Jes followed while his gaze turned to the slices of meat on the tray.

"Why do you eat meat?"

Jes cocked his head. "Well," he paused, amused at the innocence of the question. "Meat is sustenance I guess. Do you not know of the laws to make use of every part of the slaughtered animals?"

Moros laughed. "I'm a Governing God, Jes. Of course, I know of that law."

"It's a contradiction, I know," Jes replied. "But Beskermers, in some way we're no different than the animal prey in the wild. We're strong and we require certain nutrients to fight and protect. Everything we do though to feed ourselves is ethical. We also eat following the crops of the seasons. Or we do our best. Technically, I wouldn't eat so much meat at the beginning of spring. I'm more inclined to fish at this time of year."

"Fish?" Moros asked.

"Moros," Jes replied. "Why are you pressing to know what I eat?"

Moros's eyes turned away, his shoulders slumping. "I'm nervous."

"Why?"

Jes's heartbeat picked up. His hands gripped the blankets under him. It was coming. The finality of this peace and comfort.

"My mother says love can be painful," Moros murmured.

His blue eyes turned away from Jes's gaze. His hands trembled and Jes watched the wine in his mug slosh with the movement.

"But she also said that painful love doesn't always mean it's not worth fighting for."

"Moros?" Jes questioned again.

"I love you," Moros said, keeping his eyes across the room. "Fates, do I love you. I love the way your lips turn up when you're amused. I love the way your muscles flex in your forearm when you're holding me while we fly. I love your stubbornness. I love—"

Jes cut him off, pulling the mug from his hands and placing it away. Gently, he leaned against the God, pressing his back against the blankets beneath them.

"Keep going," Jes begged.

"I—" Moros cleared his throat. "I think about you. Night and Day. Every waking moment I wonder what you're doing. I imagine that body training. I hear your commanding voice bossing around your guards."

A pulse jumped between them and Jes ground his hips, determined for Moros to feel his own arousal.

"Don't distract me," Moros smiled up at him.

"Keep going," Jes said again, his hands resting beside Moros's head.

"I know you've experienced pain. I know you're scared. Fates, I'm scared. I'm scared to lose you. I'm scared for the monsters I monitor to realize how I feel about you."

Jes leaned up, the words swirling in his head.

"Monsters?" he asked.

"I get upset that you won't *claim me*..." Moros's voice trailed off. "But, ironically I understand probably more than anyone else in this fucked up world."

"Why?"

Moros stared at him. "Why what?"

"Why protect them?"

Moros shook his head. "No one can control Aamon."

Jes jolted, shocked Moros had referred to the King so casually.

"But I can keep an eye on Marek. I can try to guide him away from the madness that runs rampant in our family. I can try to remind him he owes that man nothing. That if the Fates determine him worthy of being King, that he can be better."

Jes leaned back on his hands, his chest raising and falling slowly. "Why were you in Nacht that night?"

Moros blinked before his trembling voice replied, "I saw things, Jes... I—" He took a breath. "I stopped the man I once believed had a chance at being good do depraved things. I pulled a barely breathing woman from his room while I screamed at our *King* to get out of my way. She was broken, Jesiel. Not her body but her mind."

Jes was sure his pulse had slowed as he listened to Moros.

"I went to Nacht because I was one of the observant ones at the challenge. I saw Roan holding back. I felt his powering trying to come out. So, I thought that maybe, just maybe, I could override years of him hating me and beg him to fight next time."

"I have to tell him," Jes replied. "He has to know."

Moros shook his head. "No, Jes. He knows."

"No, he doesn't," Jes snapped.

"He may not know about this instance. Fates, I wish I could burn it from my mind and memory. But Roan saw it all before any of us were willing to admit Marek was a lost cause." Moros leaned back on his hands.

"I must sit with my choices. I must accept the years I spent pushing Roan away when he longed for someone to hear his warning cries. This is my burden to bear."

"Moros," Jes leaned forward. "I can't keep this from my bonded."

Moros offered him a sad smile. "I know, my winged brute. Just don't expect anything to come from it. Aamon won't do a thing. The Fates won't step in. All you can do is encourage that coward to fight for our future."

Jes's body went rigid while the insult left Moros's lips. His wings fanned out before tucking in tightly while he rolled his shoulders, trying to shake off the instinct to fight for his bonded.

"I understand, Jes," Moros whispered.

Jes stared at him, watching his face shift to a grim expression.

"What do you understand?" he asked.

"There will always be extra people in this relationship," Moros replied, his eyes lining with tears. "We both have duties we've bound ourselves to. Responsibilities. People to protect. It can never just be *Jesiel and Moros*."

Jes's heart sank at the admission. Words and reality he'd known to be true months before this moment. It didn't prevent the sting of it all being voiced. No, he hadn't expected the pain that ripped through him.

"Where does this leave us?"

Moros turned his head while the question left Jes's lips. He leaned forward, brushing his cold hand across Jes's cheek.

"It means we make the most out of what we have. We soak in every moment together. We cherish each stolen touch, gaze, and kiss. We do everything we can to be only us when we're together. Always knowing that those who demand our loyalty could call us back at a moment's notice."

Jes held Moros's hand against his skin, emotion welling in his chest.

"That doesn't sound like a life."

"It's our life, Jesiel. Unless you can open a portal to a world where neither of us have responsibilities, this is what the Fates have given us," Moros replied, brushing his fingers across Jes's lips.

"You're a Governing God. You can have anyone," Jes countered. "What if you grow impatient with me?"

Moros pulled back, his eyes glistening with tears. "That could happen…" His voice shook. "I'm not perfect. I could one day wake up and decide I hate this life. That I want to proudly proclaim my love for you."

Jes glanced at the ground. "What if I never can? What if Roan never gains the courage? What if I fail in my duty? What if we find ourselves standing beside two rivals Fated to rule the world both on the wrong side of where they should have been?"

"If Marek becomes King," Moros paused. "If he becomes King then my duty to protect anyone he gets his hands on will become even more important than my Region."

Jes balked at the proclamation, shaking his head. "Arno should step up."

"Jes, the fact that Roan does not command you in any way is an anomaly amongst the Governing Gods. Marek has Arno on a short leash, even if your cousin wants to fight that."

Moros stood, placing his hands on his hips. "No, it's my duty. I took that role decades ago. I just never realized I would have someone else to consider down the road."

"Come here," Jes said quietly, motioning for Moros to return at his side.

Moros responded, slowly lowering himself once more and nestling into the crook of Jes's arm. His head laid on Jes's shoulder and Jes breathed out.

"Is this it then? Stolen evenings in a hidden cabin?"

Moros nodded, placing his hand on Jes's thigh. "It has to be my winged man. It has to be."

Jes held Moros tightly while the bright sun above shifted with the passing day. The food beside them went untouched and he and Moros barely moved from their position.

Every now and then Jes would glance at the man in his arms, regret pulsing through his veins. But also, gratitude for the madness that had sent him to this spot. This moment in time. Because Moros was the mirror to his soul. The air that filled his lungs. The warmth enveloping his body even when they were miles apart. He gave his love selflessly, and Jes couldn't help but wonder if he was worthy of it.

EPILOGUE

Jes stepped through the portal into Moros's private study, expecting his partner to be waiting at his desk like usual. Instead, he found the hearth unlit, the room dark, and an odd icy breeze coming through the open door.

Panic ran through Jes as he rushed toward the doors, out to the hallway of the Palace of Wintur. His body twisted back and forth, not knowing whether to run to Moros's bedroom or to the throne room.

In his frenzy, he didn't notice the quiet footsteps coming down the hall. "Calm down you brute," Riki's voice whispered.

Jes's head snapped to his cousin. Laying his trembling palms against his thigh, he cleared his throat. "Where is he?"

Riki's golden eyes gleamed with an unfamiliar mischief. "On the balcony."

Jes's heart lurched at the words. *The balcony*. Their story, their beginning had started on a balcony another Region over.

That nyight, twenty-five years before when he could no longer ignore his attraction to his icy man. When Moros had unintentionally forced himself into Jes's mind and heart, taking root with such a fury that nothing Jes did had allowed him to shake it.

Nodding his head in understanding, Jes left his grinning cousin and ran down the cold hallways of the palace.

How has it been twenty-five years?

The idea was unbelievable, really, when Jes had gone over two centuries avoiding love beyond familial bonds. Guilt rose up in his chest as his mind raced through the time he'd had Moros beside him.

In secret.

How much longer could he keep the other piece of his heart locked away from the world? When would Moros finally crack and call off their love, their bond?

Jes stopped for a moment, leaning against the cold wall beside him. Placing his hand on his heart, his tears lined his eyes.

He lived a life of lies. Of deceit. Despite having made an agreement together in a cabin twenty-four years before, he always wondered when Moros would grow impatient.

When he would lose the thread of sanity that kept Jes going each day.

He made his way through Moros's palace, heading toward the balcony overlooking Kall, only Moros wasn't there.

What was there was a pure white scroll.

When Jes picked it up, he laughed, shaking his head.

Always chasing after me, Beskermer. Come and find me. I may be naked when you get here.

Jes set the scroll down, his eyes catching the footprints heading across the balcony. With a grin, he took flight, using his advantage from the sky.

He circled the palace, his honed eyesight tracking where the footsteps led back inside.

Landing on the balcony, Jes ran back through the house, heading up the lone spire.

Where you knew the man he loved awaited.

When he shoved open the bedroom doors, he stopped in his tracks and tears lined his eyes.

Surrounding their bedroom were trinkets from the last twenty-five years. Little things Moros had appeared to save. Some Jes recognized and some he had no idea where they came from.

Moros came from his closet door, a shy grin on his face.

"Do you like it?" he asked.

Jes was across the room in an instant, gripping Moros's cheeks.

"I love you," he replied, placing a kiss on his love's lips. "I love this."

Moros pulled away. "Twenty-five years, Jesiel. Who would have imagined?"

He pointed to the table in the middle of the room and Jes grinned. "Do you want the honest answer?"

Moros shook his head while he laughed. "No, actually, I do not. Sit down."

Jes did as he was told, watching while Moros paced before him.

"What's wrong?"

Moros only shook his head. "You're distracting me."

Jes leaned back, crossing his hands over his chest while he watched Moros's hands begin to move. Then slowly, Moros turned his body toward him while snow circled around his forearms and palms.

Jes was captivated by the beauty in the way Moros's body reacted to the cold and how it flowed around him like an outer-skin.

Then he blinked when it all suddenly stopped and in Moros's hands was a sculpture of solid ice.

Jes's tears filled his eyes while he stared at the sculpture of a winged man embracing another man.

"It's us," he choked out.

Moros nodded, setting the sculpture on the table.

"It'll never melt. It'll never fade. Always and forever, Jesiel Keita. You're never getting rid of me."

Jes stared at the sculpture while his tears fell.

"I'll cherish it always," he promised.

His eyes met Moros's, and his heart swelled.

Twenty-five years.

Yet the courage in his heart was as young as the day his icy man had first appeared on that balcony. And he wondered, what would it take for that courage to take root for them both to live the life they deserved?

ACKNOWLEDGEMENTS

Writing Jes and Moros's story was quite the emotional journey for me. These are two characters who hold very special places in my heart. Many tears were cried over their love, and it was an honor to write their story and the safety they found within each other.

I want to thank my husband, for always supporting me. For the laughs. For allowing me to breakdown and cry over fictional characters I've created. And for never doubting my ability to become an author.

Thank you to the Of Fate readers. Your support and love of this world and these characters has genuinely changed my life.

Thank you to new readers, who maybe found me through this novella. Thank you for giving my world a chance, and hopefully falling in love with it in the process.

To my chaotic coven (you know who you are), thank you for the late-night laughs. Thank you for the support. Thank you for the love. I didn't expect to find such wonderful friendships, and I'm grateful for each of you.

To Sophie, my editor, and Brittany, my proofreader, thank you for supporting me. Thank you for combing through each novel and helping me make them the best they can be. You are both amazing and I wouldn't have the finished products that I do without either of you.

BE SURE TO CHECK OUT THE OTHER NOVELLAS IN THE

FROM
LOATHING
TO LOVERS
NOVELLA COLLECTION

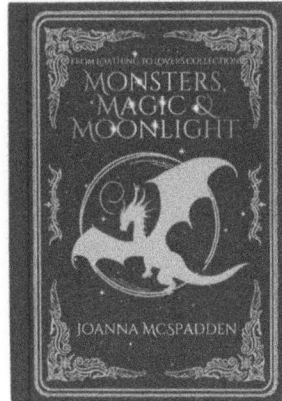

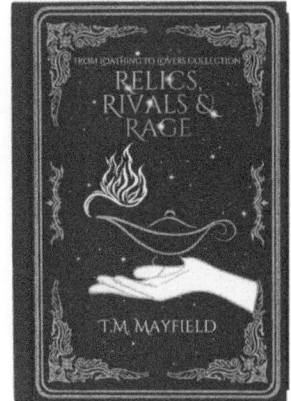

SOUL, SUN & STARS
K.M. DAVIDSON

FEATHERS, FROST & FATE
C.K. BLOOMING

DECEPTION, DEATH & THE DIVINE
LINDSEY N. RHODEN

HAVEN, HALLOW & HIGHBORN
JESSA GREY

MONSTERS, MAGIC & MOONLIGHT
JOANNA MCSPADDEN

RELICS, RIVALS & RAGE
T.M. MAYFIELD

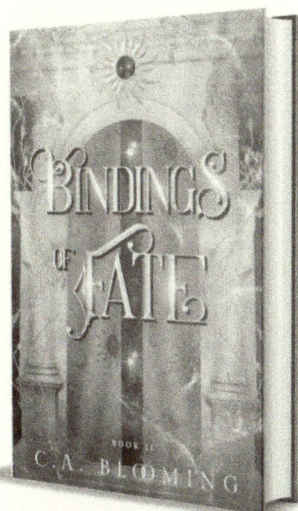

About the Author

Courtney (C.A.) Blooming is an adult fantasy author. She began writing her debut novel, Threads of Fate, in July 2023. As of February 2025, she has three published books, with multiple projects underway.

Outside of the safety of books and stories, she is a wife and mother to three children. She works full-time in client success management. You can generally find her sitting in front of a computer working on her never-ending task list, or in a family snuggle pile with her husband and children.

For updates regarding upcoming publications, or to follow Courtney's author journey, you can find her on the social media platforms below, or through her website:

Website: cablooming.com

Instagram: @cablooming

Tiktok: @cablooming

www.ingramcontent.com/pod-product-compliance
Ingram Content Group UK Ltd.
Pitfield, Milton Keynes, MK11 3LW, UK
UKHW031836210225
455389UK00015B/103/J

9 781964 087092